DUSTY AYRES AND HIS BATTLE BIRDS:
THE BLACK AVENGER

DUSTY AYRES and his BATTLE BIRDS

THE BLACK AVENGER

By Robert Sidney Bowen

ALTUS PRESS • 2017

CHAPTER 1
MIDNIGHT DEATH

S LOUCHING BACK lazily in the mess lounge chair, Dusty grinned over the top of his drink at the heavy-set figure of Second Lieutenant (ex-Sergeant) Biff Bolton.

"Well, Biff," he grunted, "how's it feel to do loops with H.S. Group Seven?" The former non-com pilot returned the grin and swizzled the ice around in his half empty glass.

"Couldn't be better! Only—well, it seems funny to have a bar on my shoulder straps instead of chevrons on my sleeve. And I haven't quite got used to taking salutes instead of giving them. Sure was white of you, skipper, recommending me for a commission."

Dusty made a face.

"Forget it! You rated it—and how! We need more like you in this man's argument."

"Right!" spoke up Curly Brooks, seated on Bolton's left. "But you were a sucker to take him up on his offer, Biff! This guy, Ayres, will work your pants off—and then not even pay for the drinks. I know him, see? Two bits says he doesn't stand for the next one, and it's his turn."

"Something I've been meaning to tell you, Biff," said Dusty seriously. "Always remember that the war does queer things to some chaps, and it's best just to humor them. Take Curly, for instance. Why, before he crashed and hit his head that time, he

1

by Robert Sidney Bowen

really had the makings of a pilot. But since then—well, you get the idea. It's really a shame and—hey!"

Dusty was too late. He tried desperately to dodge Curly's drink sliding across the table, and failed fifty per cent. The glass slid off the edge of the table and drenched his left side with Scotch and soda. And as he tried to squirm back on the chair, Curly calmly reached over and appropriated his pal's drink.

"To your good health, Captain Ayres," he grinned, raising the glass. "If I were a spy I'd tell the Blacks to use Scotch and soda instead of bullets—then they might score a hit on you now and then."

"Why, you long-eared bum!" roared Dusty scrambling to his feet. "Gimme that glass!"

He lunged forward, both hands outstretched. With a quick motion Curly jumped back. But his left foot tangled up with his right, and refused to become untangled in the split second of time allowed. The result was that Curly, still clutching Dusty's drink, went over flat on his back on the floor and received the entire contents of the glass square in the face.

Unable to check his lunge, Dusty went sprawling on top of him. And in the next second they were rolling over and over on the floor, tightly locked in each other's arms.

"Hey, you two! Come up for air!" At the sound of the shouting voice they relaxed, let go of each other and blinked up at the figure of Major Drake, standing over them. The C.O.'s face was stern, but there was a twinkle in his eye. He shook his head slowly from side to side.

"Not that I care whether you two break each other's necks!" he grunted. "But damned if I'll let you waste my perfectly good Scotch. On your feet, you Indians—there's work to be done!"

With the remnants of the drink still dripping from their grinning faces the pair got up and smoothed out their uniforms.

"Swell, major," said Dusty. "What's the job this time?"

For answer the C.O. held out a radiogram.

"Just decoded it," he said. "It's for you."

Dusty took it and glanced at the typed words:

est was lost as the speaker unit made a crashing sound.
most like an explosion of some sort. Dusty's hand flew
ial knob and turned it a shade to the left. A piercing
ortal agony blasted out of the cabin speaker unit.
help us… send help, quick… it's wiping us all out. Can't
much longer. Help… oh God, here it is… it's reached
. oh my God!"

DD-CURDLING cry of stark terror—then a sharp
absolute silence. At the same instant the red signal
ked out for the second time in as many minutes. But
ond before it did, Dusty's eyes had flashed to the
ectional-finder needle.

bit of calculation placed the strange station some
n hundred miles due south of his position. Snapping
ssion he grabbed up the transmitter tube.

station just broadcasting on wave-length Four-
he shouted. "What is your area reading? What is
ocation number?"

s he repeated the call, and then sat waiting breath-
lued to the red signal light bulb on the panel. Four
gged by, but the bulb didn't blink once.

ral States station, kid," suggested Curly in excited
must have picked up those signals."
lded and put through the call.

et emergency signals on Four-Nine-Six?" he asked.
r unit crackled words back immediately.
e couldn't make anything of them. Couldn't even
cation. What about you?"

Major Drake, C.O.
H.S. Group 7
Instruct Captain Ayres to select two other pilots of your
Group and report to me at Ex-127 at once.
Bradley
Chief of Air Force Staff.

"Ex-one-two-seven?" echoed Dusty, frowning. "That's the
experimental depot at Cleveland. What the hell—he making
us test pilots, now?"

The C.O. shrugged.

"Search me," he grunted. "But pick your two, and shove off
in the cabin job. I told the flight sergeant to warm her up on
the way over."

"Right, sir," nodded Dusty, shoving the radiogram in his
pocket. Then to Bolton, "Want to come along, Biff?"

The former non-com's grin was a mile long. "You bet!" he
gulped.

Dusty turned his head so that Curly couldn't see, and winked
at Bolton.

"Now let's see," he murmured slowly, "who else could we take
along?"

"I'll muss your homely mug for that crack, later!" growled
Curly starting for the door. "Come on, you two—shake it up!"

"Oh yes, Curly Brooks!" grunted Dusty in mock surprise, as
he and Bolton followed the lean pilot through the door. "I
believe he did learn to fly once."

As the door slammed shut on them, Major Drake heaved a
long sigh and poured himself a drink.

"Damn fools—bless 'em!" he said into the glass. "Wish to hell they were twins, each of 'em!"

ONCE OUTSIDE the mess lounge, the three pilots dropped their rough-house stuff and walked quickly over to a biplane cabin job waiting in front of the lighted hangars, prop ticking over. Two minutes later, Dusty, at the controls, sent it streaking down the flood-lighted takeoff runway, and then pulled it up into the night sky.

Holding the nose heavenward he climbed to thirty thousand, then leveled off and set a dead-on robot course southwest toward the experimental depot at Cleveland. Up to then neither of them had spoken. And it was Curly who first broke the silence. He leaned forward from his double seat shared with Bolton and touched Dusty on the arm.

"What's your guess, kid?"

"Guess about what?"

"Guess about what Bradley wants," said Curly. "Hell, it can't be test jobs, can it?"

Dusty shrugged, took time out to check course and direction, just on general principles.

"Never can tell," he answered eventually. "I heard a rumor a week ago that Air Force Engineering was working on a new design."

"Better than the Flash?" spoke up Bolton.

Dusty shrugged again.

"Some crate, if it is," he said. "The Flash is aces enough for me."

Silence settled over the trio again. In the dim glow of the

ceiling light they sat like three stat and each mulling over the same qu of air force staff want now?

Fifteen minutes dragged by, and up straight in their seats. The red s was blinking rapidly.

With a quick motion of his h and turned the wave-length dia unit crackled sound. But that v unintelligible sound at that.

Dusty cursed softly, and fid control. But it didn't help at all. unit simply increased or decre sort of sing-songy in quality. stop at regular intervals, and bit of it could be linked up v

"What the hell?" exclaim the broadcasting station?"

There was no answer fo Biff Bolton made an atter rowed, they sat listening stopped altogether and th

"Off the air, anyway," sa switch.

But he didn't touch it. this time the cabin spea

"Emergency all statio all available air units o

The It was a to the d cry of m "God hold out us—we. A BLO click and light blin a split se station dir A rapid five to seve on transmi "Calling Nine-Six!" your map l Four tim lessly, eyes g minutes dra "Try Cen tones. "They Dusty no "Did you g The speake "Yes. But w get the area l

"The same," Dusty said. "But according to my directional finder it's somewhere in the K-Four area. North of Louisville, I'd say."

"Thanks," crackled the speaker unit. "Sign off to clear air, while we try to contact, will you?"

"Signing off," repeated Dusty, and he flipped down the switch.

Both Curly and Biff had hitched forward on their seats, and the eyes they fixed on Dusty as he turned toward them were just as questioning as his own.

He shrugged, made a face.

"Hell's popping somewhere," he said. "But, that singing sound—I've heard it before, but damned if I can remember where!"

"Thinking the same thing!" nodded Curly. "Just after the start of the war—"

"Hey, look! The light's blinking!"

Biff Bolton's voice drowned out whatever Curly was going to say. The signal light was blinking furiously. In one sweeping motion of his hand, Dusty snapped on reception and spun the dial. Reaction of the speaker unit was practically instantaneous.

"A-Six... A-Six... A-Six! Get out of the air! Get out of the air! Land at once and report position to Ex-One-Two-Seven, by ground wire. Get out of the air at once!"

"A-Six? That's your code number, Dusty!"

Dusty hardly heard Curly's shouting voice. He was staring at the cabin speaker unit. There was no doubt about the owner of that voice. General Bradley was ordering him out of the air.

He started to snap on transmission for a check-back, but

something—a sudden tingling sensation at the back of his neck—stopped him. Instead he reached up and flipped off the ceiling light, plunging the cabin into darkness.

"What's the idea?" spoke up Bolton's voice in the darkness.

Busty didn't answer at once. He leaned forward and strained his eyes out into the black heavens.

"A hunch," he grunted finally. "I don't think we're alone upstairs."

The words were as a signal for the other two to press their faces against the cabin windows and stare out into the darkness. For several seconds silence hung over them like a heavy curtain. Then suddenly, Bolton grunted aloud.

"Take a look up there to the left!" he snapped out. "Is that exhaust flames?"

Dusty and Curly screwed around and peered up as directed. They both saw it at the same time—a faint trail of pale purple sparks describing a circular pattern in the heavens. At times the eerie sight was brilliant with color, and then it would suddenly fade out until it was almost entirely gone. Then like dying embers fanned by a stiff wind, it would flare up again. Finally, it faded out altogether, and did not reappear again.

Turning front, Dusty risked the cowl light low enough to check compass and roller map.

"The hell with landing!" he said to the others. "We're close enough to Cleveland to power dive in. I think our best bet is to find out from Bradley what the hell everything's all about."

"Check!" echoed the other two in the same breath. "Let's go!"

And a power dive it was! Engine wide open, Dusty sent the ship thundering down through the night. Just north of Cleveland a brace of searchlights sprang into being, picked him up, then winked out as those on the ground spotted the markings on the ship.

Three minutes later he streaked over the edge of Experimental Depot Field No. 127, fish-tailed to cut forward speed, and settled down to a perfect three-point. And in less than no time after that he had taxied up to the hangar line and was legging out.

No sooner had his feet touched the tarmac, than steel fingers swung him around. The voice of General Bradley cut at him like the lash of a whip.

"You young fool, Ayres! You might have been killed. Didn't you get my radio order to land at once?"

"Yes, sir," nodded Dusty, gently but firmly easing himself loose from the other's grasp. "I did, and here we are. What's up?"

Dusty's question, or perhaps his unruffled manner, drained anger from the general's face. The chief of air force staff bit his lip, started to speak, and then seemed to cut it off with a shake of his head. He made a jerking motion with his hand, and turned on his heel.

"Follow me, the three of you," he flung over his shoulder.

WITH THAT he went stalking down the tarmac. He led them past the field mess lounge and over to the office shack. Not stopping to knock, he barged right inside.

As Dusty entered his first glance was of a thin-faced air force colonel bent over a radio-phone on the desk. And his second glance was of a huddled uniformed figure slumped down in one corner. Too many times had Dusty seen corpses not to instantly realize that here was another one.

He shot a questioning glance at Bradley, but the chief of A.F. staff wasn't even looking at him. His eyes were riveted upon the man at the radio-phone. And then that officer, phones clamped to both ears, began to talk rapidly.

"Yes? What's that?... Wiped out?... Good God, impossible! The ground detectors—didn't they pick up something?... Oh, I see. Wiped out too, eh? Well, H.Q. orders, Springer, to get everything available there, immediately. Everything needed, understand?... Yes, yes, Intelligence is working at both ends. Our man didn't talk—eh?... Yes, shot himself. Keep your wavelength open, direct. Signing off!"

The thin-faced officer slipped the phones from his ears, twisted a couple of dials on the panel, and then looked at General Bradley.

"The first report was correct, sir," he said in a heavy voice. "Wiped out—everything! Not a living thing left. Springer's on his way there, now. Reporting back later."

The chief of air force staff received the message in frowning silence. As a matter of fact, he maintained the silence for several minutes. Dusty stood it as long as he could. Then he stepped across the room and touched the senior officer on the arm.

"Mind telling me what's happened, sir?" he asked quietly.

Bradley stared at him, as though seeing him for the first time.

Major Drake, C.O.

H.S. Group 7

Instruct Captain Ayres to select two other pilots of your Group and report to me at Ex-127 at once.

Bradley

Chief of Air Force Staff.

"Ex-one-two-seven?" echoed Dusty, frowning. "That's the experimental depot at Cleveland. What the hell—he making us test pilots, now?"

The C.O. shrugged.

"Search me," he grunted. "But pick your two, and shove off in the cabin job. I told the flight sergeant to warm her up on the way over."

"Right, sir," nodded Dusty, shoving the radiogram in his pocket. Then to Bolton, "Want to come along, Biff?"

The former non-com's grin was a mile long. "You bet!" he gulped.

Dusty turned his head so that Curly couldn't see, and winked at Bolton.

"Now let's see," he murmured slowly, "who else could we take along?"

"I'll muss your homely mug for that crack, later!" growled Curly starting for the door. "Come on, you two—shake it up!"

"Oh yes, Curly Brooks!" grunted Dusty in mock surprise, as he and Bolton followed the lean pilot through the door. "I believe he did learn to fly once."

As the door slammed shut on them, Major Drake heaved a long sigh and poured himself a drink.

"Damn fools—bless 'em!" he said into the glass. "Wish to hell they were twins, each of 'em!"

ONCE OUTSIDE the mess lounge, the three pilots dropped their rough-house stuff and walked quickly over to a biplane cabin job waiting in front of the lighted hangars, prop ticking over. Two minutes later, Dusty, at the controls, sent it streaking down the flood-lighted takeoff runway, and then pulled it up into the night sky.

Holding the nose heavenward he climbed to thirty thousand, then leveled off and set a dead-on robot course southwest toward the experimental depot at Cleveland. Up to then neither of them had spoken. And it was Curly who first broke the silence. He leaned forward from his double seat shared with Bolton and touched Dusty on the arm.

"What's your guess, kid?"

"Guess about what?"

"Guess about what Bradley wants," said Curly. "Hell, it can't be test jobs, can it?"

Dusty shrugged, took time out to check course and direction, just on general principles.

"Never can tell," he answered eventually. "I heard a rumor a week ago that Air Force Engineering was working on a new design."

"Better than the Flash?" spoke up Bolton.

Dusty shrugged again.

"Some crate, if it is," he said. "The Flash is aces enough for me."

Silence settled over the trio again. In the dim glow of the

ceiling light they sat like three statues, staring unseeing ahead, and each mulling over the same question—what did the chief of air force staff want now?

Fifteen minutes dragged by, and then as one man they jerked up straight in their seats. The red signal light on the radio panel was blinking rapidly.

With a quick motion of his hand, Dusty flipped on contact and turned the wave-length dial. Instantly, the cabin speaker unit crackled sound. But that was all it was, just sound—and unintelligible sound at that.

Dusty cursed softly, and fiddled with the dial and volume control. But it didn't help at all. The sound emitted by the speaker unit simply increased or decreased at his touch. It was clear and sort of sing-songy in quality. Yet at the same time it seemed to stop at regular intervals, and then continue again. But not one bit of it could be linked up with syllables of spoken words.

"What the hell?" exclaimed Curly. "Is our set haywire, or is the broadcasting station?"

There was no answer for that one, and neither Dusty nor Biff Bolton made an attempt. Brows furrowed, and eyes narrowed, they sat listening to the strange sound. Suddenly, it stopped altogether and the red signal blinked out.

"Off the air, anyway," said Dusty as he reached for the contact switch.

But he didn't touch it. The red signal light blinked again, and this time the cabin speaker unit crackled out crisp words.

"Emergency all stations! Send help immediately! Concentrate all available air units over—"

The rest was lost as the speaker unit made a crashing sound. It was almost like an explosion of some sort. Dusty's hand flew to the dial knob and turned it a shade to the left. A piercing cry of mortal agony blasted out of the cabin speaker unit.

"God help us… send help, quick… it's wiping us all out. Can't hold out much longer. Help… oh God, here it is… it's reached us—we… oh my God!"

A BLOOD-CURDLING cry of stark terror—then a sharp click and absolute silence. At the same instant the red signal light blinked out for the second time in as many minutes. But a split second before it did, Dusty's eyes had flashed to the station directional-finder needle.

A rapid bit of calculation placed the strange station some five to seven hundred miles due south of his position. Snapping on transmission he grabbed up the transmitter tube.

"Calling station just broadcasting on wave-length Four-Nine-Six!" he shouted. "What is your area reading? What is your map location number?"

Four times he repeated the call, and then sat waiting breathlessly, eyes glued to the red signal light bulb on the panel. Four minutes dragged by, but the bulb didn't blink once.

"Try Central States station, kid," suggested Curly in excited tones. "They must have picked up those signals."

Dusty nodded and put through the call.

"Did you get emergency signals on Four-Nine-Six?" he asked.

The speaker unit crackled words back immediately.

"Yes. But we couldn't make anything of them. Couldn't even get the area location. What about you?"

hrough his veins like liquid fire. For one hellish instant every-hing in the room became a whirling blur—a whirling hazy blur of deep crimson. With a mighty effort he managed to get a semblance of control on his temper.

"Then you mean," he sputtered out, "that instead of trying to beat hell out of a bunch of rats who are trying to wreck this country, I'm supposed to sit back like a little tin god on wheels for others to look at, and marvel?"

He had sense enough to stop short as Bradley raised a silencing hand.

"You're looking at it in the wrong light, captain," he said quietly. "You will still have plenty of work to do—useful work. In the past, you have refused all promotion. You have been content with your Congressional assignment as Special Contact Officer to the combined forces of the U.S. Government. Well, the time has come to force promotion upon you, for the best interests of all concerned. You will be assigned to a high-ranking position on my staff, and with your assistance, based on experience and concrete knowledge, we shall be able to build a more effective air force than we have at the present time."

From out of a thick fog of bitter disappointment and rage, Dusty heard his own voice.

"And if I still refuse, sir?"

He saw the corners of Bradley's mouth twitch. Saw the officer's chin come out a bit.

"It is not whether you will refuse, or not, captain! It is an order that you will see fit to obey. Believe me, I sympathize with your personal feelings. And I admire you for wanting to con-

"Everything!" he suddenly boomed out. "Everything! God knows what it is! And God knows how we're going to stop it!"

He started tugging savagely at one side of his bristling mustache. Dusty gave him a couple of minutes to cool off. Then he tried again.

"Yes, sir. But what happened?"

"Eh?" ejaculated the other, coming out of his brooding trance. "Oh yes! The Louisville Base was completely destroyed an hour ago. Not a thing remains for a radius of almost ten miles. Completely laid waste!"

Dusty felt little feet of ice dancing up and down his spine.

"How, sir? What did it?"

If the chief of A.F. staff's look could have killed, the pilot would have dropped dead right then and there.

"How?" he thundered. "If I knew, do you think I'd be standing here doing nothing? We don't know. That's what we're trying to find out."

Dusty swallowed hard and succeeded in keeping his voice even toned.

"But you must have some idea, sir," he persisted. "Was it a ground explosion, or an air raid, or what?"

Bradley's face went beet-red with exasperated rage, then suddenly he relaxed and sighed heavily.

"We do not know, Captain Ayres!" he said. "We only got scraps of an emergency message from that area. We could only check-back as far as K-Six, fifty miles this side. They flew over the area. You just heard Colonel Randal, here, give me their report. Everything wiped out—and nobody knows how, or why!"

Dusty started to speak again, hesitated. Finally he said: "Tell me, sir. What caused you to radio that order for me to land?"

The other started, as though suddenly remembering something. He swung around and pointed at the dead man crumpled up in the corner.

"That!" he snapped. "He was assistant radio officer at this field. We caught him signaling to someone that you were in the air and on your way down. He was brought into this office for questioning—but the devil fooled us. Had a tiny derringer hidden under his left armpit. We couldn't stop him in time. He shot himself."

As though to prove his words, Bradley swung back and pointed at the desk. On top of it was a pearl-handled derringer. Dusty gave it a glance, turned his eyes back to the general's face.

"Who was he signaling to?" he asked. "And how much did he get through?"

The other shrugged.

"Can't answer the first," he said gruffly. "Colonel Randal caught him in the middle of the message. He hadn't sent out this area map reading number yet. Just starting to. I didn't care to take chances, so I ordered you to land. You're a marked man, you know, Captain Ayres. The Blacks will never forgive you the loss of the Hawk. And we do not intend to let you get yourself killed!"

Dusty grinned.

"I wouldn't worry about that, sir," he said. "I'm r And I'll take my chances of going on living."

The senior officer fixed him with a steady gaze shook his head.

"That is exactly where you are wrong, Captain A₁ in a voice that was like steel against steel. "Beginnir this very minute, you will take no more chances of by the Black Invaders!"

CHAPTER 2
LIGHTNING STRIKES TW

RIGID FROM head to foot, Dusty stood sta at General Bradley. At first he did not und then is the words came blasting home to him, be g;

"You—you mean—" he started to choke out.

"Yes, I mean exactly *that!*" came the sharp answ a question of your own personal desire for life or de It is a matter of morale—the morale of thousand been inspired by the fine things you have done. Yo action would be a serious blow. We cannot affo enemy is pressing us hard, and every little thing in no matter how small—counts triple. You have buil unparalleled in the history of the air force. And t that record upon others is of greater value to our anything else you could possibly accomplish. Your hands of the enemy would reduce that value to nil

Dusty's heart pounded against his ribs and the b

tinue on throwing yourself, and might, in the path of the enemy. But you've done enough of that. We cannot afford to let you do it once too often!"

Dusty's voice was a cross between a growl and a savage moan.

"Then—" he began, and stopped. "Then you ordered me down here, to tell me all this?"

Bradley shrugged.

"Partly," he said. "But the main reason was to show you something—to get your expert opinion and advice upon a matter that we had hoped was a complete secret."

The general paused, turned his eyes toward the dead man in the corner.

"But I don't feel so sure about that, now," he murmured, as though talking to himself. "No, I most decidedly do not feel so sure."

With a shrug and a sigh, he turned back to Colonel Randal, who still sat like marble back of the desk.

"If you get anything, colonel," he said. "Call me at once in Hangar X. And don't leave this office for an instant."

"Very good, sir," replied the other stiffly.

Bradley nodded, swept the three pilots with a single glance. "Please come with me, gentlemen."

Body like sagging lead, Dusty was only dully conscious of his feet moving in the wake of the air force chief. It was as though he were sleep walking in the midst of some hellish nightmare, and all about him scores of grinning demons, were screaming—"You're through! A little tin god! You're through! You're through!"

"Hold it, kid! Easy! We'll find a way out!"

Like a spring suddenly being released, Dusty jerked his head around and blinked into the lean face of Curly Brooks. The tall pilot was gripping his arm tightly, and nodding his head up and down. His voice was low; too low for Bradley, five paces ahead, to hear.

"Chin up, kid! Staff gets that way, sometimes. Just hold your horses. We'll wangle it somehow."

Dusty forced a smile to his lips that he did not feel inside. Good old Curly! Right shoulder to shoulder with him, in everything—a fight or a frolic or whatnot! He reached up and gripped his pal's hand.

"Thanks," he grunted.

SPIRITS UP a slight fraction, he put his shoulders back, and followed General Bradley down the entire length of the tarmac. At the end, the senior officer turned the corner, and walked toward a low-roofed stone building, set back some seventy-five to one hundred yards behind the main row of hangars.

As they neared it, Dusty saw that a cordon of armed guards completely surrounded the building. And each man's rifle was held at the alert; its owner ready to jerk the trigger at an instant's notice. They were still twenty-five yards from the building, when at least a dozen rifles became trained dead upon them, and the order rang out sharp and clear.

"Halt! Stand right where you are!" All four did that little thing, instinctively, and watched a slim infantry lieutenant advance toward them. A flashlight in his hand sprang into life,

THE BLACK AVENGER

It was a perfect airplane,

if there ever was one.

and its beam flooded General Bradley's face with white light. A split second later it slid off and "spotted" the three pilots, one after the other. "These officers with you, sir?"

"Yes, lieutenant. My compliments, on your alertness."

"Simply my orders, sir," replied the lieutenant, still keeping his flashlight beam swinging from one to the other. "Now, if you'll just proceed ahead of me, sir."

General Bradley turned to the others, beckoned with a jerk of his head, and then walked toward the stone building.

It was then that Dusty suddenly noticed that the building did not contain a single window of any sort, and that its wall gave the appearance of great thickness. Further speculation was cut off short as they were brought up by a solid row of rifles.

"General Bradley and three officers, sir," Dusty heard the young lieutenant's voice behind him.

A figure stepped through the row of rifles, stopped in front of General Bradley and saluted smartly. Dusty recognized him instantly. The man was Major Pratt, former C.O. of the Dayton test field, and designer of the X-Rayoscope plane. The officer said but three words to Bradley.

"This way, sir."

Instantly the row of rifles parted, and Pratt led them over to a solid metal door. From his tunic pocket he withdrew a key, fitted it in the lock and twisted. There was a dull thump of a tumbler falling into place, and then the major swung the heavy door open. Beyond it was a limitless void of solid darkness. But, a moment later there was the click of a switch, and a tiny yellow glow flooded a narrow passageway that slanted down slightly.

"Watch your step, gentlemen," Major Pratt's voice drifted back. "There's a hand rail, here on the right."

There was. Gripping it, Dusty and his two pals followed Bradley and Pratt down the stone floor passageway. At the bottom the major unlocked another door, shoved it open and flipped on a brace of switches. Instantly, everything was bathed in glaring white light. To Dusty, it was as though he had stepped from the darkness of midnight into the brilliance of high noon.

At first everything was blinding. And then as the retina of his eyes focused to the sudden change of light, objects took on definite shape and outline. They were standing in a great square room, at least two hundred feet square.

Along the walls were machines of every possible description—drill presses, stampers, lathes and cutters, moulds and jig machines, welding apparatus and scalding vats. And from the girdered, domed ceiling suspended a dozen different cranes and block and pulley tackles. In fact, it was almost like the prize showroom of a great industrial, mechanical and electrical show.

But to all of that, Dusty gave but a fleeting glance. What caught and held his gaze transfixed, were three objects resting on the floor—three beautifully streamlined, Diesel-powered, high-lift wing monoplane pursuits.

From their high-finned tail sections to their arrow-head snouts they represented to Dusty the very acme of all things aeronautical. He forgot everything save their indescribable beauty. He forgot the mysterious disaster which had befallen Louisville Base. He forgot the eerie and slightly familiar sound that he and his pals had heard over the radio. In fact, he even forgot that he was no longer to be an active air scrapper. Everything faded in the presence of the three ships.

He walked over to the nearest one. Close proximity simply doubled his admiration, and sent his airman's blood pounding through his body.

The engine was of the four bank X arranged type, its cowling being faired into the spinners of the double torque counteracting propellers fitted with constant speed gears. The wing, which tapered in both plan and form, was so set into the rear top of the engine cowl that it seemed to be an integral part of the fuselage itself. It was practically impossible to tell where the center section of the wing ended and the burnished fuselage cowling began.

In the side recesses of the X engine two Brownings were fitted; only the tip of the muzzle showing. And in the leading edge of the top wing, one on either side of the center section, was another Browning of slightly larger calibre. The gun itself was entirely enclosed in the wing, the mouth of the barrel being only a small hole, that could very easily miss the eye.

From the rear of the center section of the wing the top of the fuselage sloped slightly upward to a point about three feet in front of the tail fin. At that point was the cockpit. The cowl was of three-ply non-shatterable glass, and fitted together in three curving orange peel sections. The headrest was virtually the rudder post.

Yet so perfectly streamlined and "sun-fish" shaped was the cockpit, that it actually appeared to be no thicker than the rudder itself. In fact, looking at it from the side, the cockpit looked as though it were an integral part of the fin.

Behind and slightly below the center of thrust were stubby, fish-tail elevators fitted to a narrow triangular strip that by a great stretch of the imagination could be called a tail plane. The entire craft rested on small fat air wheels, all of which were fitted with retractable gear, leaving the bottom of the fuselage a perfect streamlined curve.

WITHOUT BOTHERING to climb into the cockpit, Dusty knew that the craft had been so designed as to give maximum vision possible. From the pit, the high-lift single wing presented no more vision obstruction than a heavy line. And the vision obstructed by the triangular tail plane was practically negligible. Vision to the rear was also perfect as the three part orange peel cowl bulged out sufficient for the pilot to lean slightly to the side and see whatever was directly behind him. In fact, the only "blind spot," if it could be called such, was that presented by the forward part of the fuselage, and the engine. But even then, a slight tap on the stick to either side would enable the pilot to see everything forward and below him.

A perfect airplane, if there ever could be a perfect airplane.

"Like it, Ayres?"

Dusty turned to look into the grinning face of Major Pratt.

"Like it?" he gulped. "My God, I still think that I'm dreaming!"

The other chuckled, reached out a hand and slid it along the burnished metal side of the fuselage.

"It's a dream all right," he said. "But, a real one, however. Been wanting to design this for months, but other things kept me tied up. Here she is, though—and she'll bring plenty of hell to the Blacks, or I miss my guess."

As the man spoke the last, Dusty suddenly remembered, and his heart slid down into his boots. Instinctively, he half turned. General Bradley, Curly and Biff were standing directly behind him. The two pilots had eyes only for the plane, but the Chief of A.F. Staff was smiling at him.

"I guess these will surprise the Blacks, eh, Ayres?" he said.

"Yes, sir," said Dusty simply, and stood waiting.

Bradley frowned slightly, licked his lips.

"As you have probably guessed, from the armed guard and everything," he suddenly said, "this has been kept a very close secret since its inception. Even the men who built the plane have been housed in separate barracks and refused any association with their friends. In other words, with these planes, and many more like them, of course, we hope to obtain complete mastery of the air!"

The senior officer paused, perhaps for emphasis. Dusty said nothing. Though he realized that he was seeing the almost perfect airplane, he knew quite well that no one type of ship could possibly gain complete mastery of the air. However, it was Bradley's party—and he had something on his mind besides glowing praise for Pratt's latest design.

"The reason I ordered you three gentlemen to report here," the general went on presently, "was for testing purposes. Neither of these planes has been in the air. On paper, they fly better than anything else we have. But I want you three pilots to test them out thoroughly. If the tests meet with your satisfaction, these planes will become the nucleus of a great U.S. air fleet. That fleet will be a roving one—under your command, Ayres."

Dusty's heart leaped. Then Bradley continued.

"The air leader will be a pilot you suggest, Ayres. He will operate in the air according to plans that you and the rest of the air force staff work out. But, to avoid a too-many-cooks idea, he will be directly responsible to you. In other words, this special fleet will be under your ground command, just as all the units and groups are under my ground command. Of course, I need not add that you will share in credit due them."

Credit due them!

Dusty's blood boiled, and a red haze of berserk recklessness started to film his eyes. A torrent of hot, bitter words rushed up out of his throat, but they did not leave his lips. Curly Brooks had edged close, and the warning nudge against his leg made Dusty stop in time. He sucked in a deep breath, swallowed hard.

"Very good, sir," he said. Then with a sideward glance at the ships, "I don't think that you need worry about the outcome of the tests. It's my guess that they'll fly even better in the air than they did on paper. When do you want us to start testing?"

Bradley and Pratt exchanged glances.

"At once," said the general. "Tonight, in fact. As a precautionary measure, none but armed guards is on the field tonight. The sooner you pass on the ship, the better. Plans have been arranged for twenty-five of these planes to be ready for service within forty-eight hours from the time these three are accepted. Others will follow, just as rapidly. Originally, I had planned for the tests to be made tomorrow, but—well, I think it best to test them tonight and get them away from this field."

There was no necessity for the senior officer to explain the reason for the last. Everyone knew it. In short, the reason was the dead Black Invader spy in the field office. Had he got word of these planes through to his countrymen? The answer they did not know.

"Assuming tests are okay, where do you wish us to fly the ships?" Dusty asked his chief.

The general started to speak, then bit his lip.

"I'll radio you in code, later," he said.

Dusty shrugged.

"Very good, sir," he said. Then turning to Major Pratt, "How do we get them out?"

The designer grinned.

"Very simple," he said. "And not piece by piece, as it must seem."

Walking over to the wall he pressed a button. A moment later the door, through which they all had entered, opened and a dozen greaseballs came inside, clicked heels and saluted smartly.

"We're taking them out, Barnes," said Major Pratt to the only non-com in the group. "Get going."

WITHOUT A word the group of greaseballs snapped into action. Three of them maneuvered electric dollies into place. Three more hoisted the tail of each ship up and fitted it into the dollie receiver. The others went over to the end wall and began turning cranks and throwing switches.

To Dusty's amazement the wall seemed to split across the middle, and the lower half slowly sank downward until it was flush with the floor. Beyond the opening was a wide shallow ramp leading up to the level of the ground outside.

"Well, I'll be damned!" grunted Dusty. "Is that fancy?"

"Yes," replied Major Pratt. "But necessary. This is one place those damn Blacks can't reach. It's bomb proof, gas proof, and everything else proof. After losing my first experimental designs by bombs, and so forth, I'm taking no more chances. So I had this place specially constructed. Could work here for weeks, with the Blacks all around us. As a matter of fact, I believe that you could even take off one of these ships right from here—zip right through the opening and up the ramp into the air."

"Maybe," Dusty smiled at the other's enthusiasm. "But first I think we'll try it from the ground outside. It will—"

The sharp clang of a gong on the wall drowned out the rest. As one man they all turned and stared at a small red light just under the gong. It was blinking rapidly. Major Pratt started over, but Bradley stopped him.

"I'll take it, major," he said. "I think it's for me."

Lifting a small inter-building phone out of its cradle, the general put his lips to the transmitter.

"Bradley," he grunted.

What the voice at the other end said, those watching the general could not hear. But they did see him stiffen rigid—saw the blood rush to his face and his eyelids open wide.

"What?... What?" he yelled back. "It's what—Gone, you say? Destroyed? Oh my God—that devil got word through then.... Yes, yes—order all bases to keep a sharp lookout. Don't take chances on anything. Damn them to hell!"

The chief of air force staff emphasized the last by practically throwing the instrument back into its cradle. When he turned and walked back to the group, his eyes held a look of baffled hopelessness as they became transfixed on Major Pratt's face.

"Damn it, Pratt!" he thundered. "Damn their rotten souls to hell!"

"Yes, sir. What's happened?"

"Happened?" the other roared. "J Four factory depot was completely destroyed half an hour ago. Wiped out—just like Louisville Base. Not a damn thing left. Randal got it from J Area H.Q. over code radio."

The major reeled back as though he had been dealt a smashing blow on the chest. A wild expression of utter disbelief seeped into his eyes. And his mouth sagged open foolishly.

"You—you—?" he gulped out. "J Four destroyed? All those ships are—"

"Yes," nodded Bradley sadly, as words failed the other. "That rat spy must have got word through before Randal caught him. They picked J Four first—every part of those twenty-five ships, like these, waiting to be assembled as soon as tests were completed, has been reduced to nothing. Nothing but charred, smoking earth, Randal said. And God knows how!"

CHAPTER 3
THE FLAMING RAIN

A S THE truth slowly sank home, the features of Major Pratt's face twitched violently. Then, suddenly, he spun clear around with a savage curse.

"Barnes!" he bellowed. "Barnes! Dollie them back in, at once. Roll up that door quick. Start the air rectifiers. Swing in the sealing lugs. We're due for a raid!"

"Yes sir!" the non-com snapped, and ran over toward the ram, where the last machine was being slowly dollied up onto hard ground.

General Bradley stared hard at Pratt.

"What the devil, Pratt?" he barked. "J Four is over a thousand miles from here! There are tests to be made tonight!"

The former C.O. of Dayton test field gestured violently.

"I don't care if J Four is a million miles away, general!" he shouted. "I'm not going to let those devils get these three ships. I'll park them here until the war ends if I have to. I've put everything into them, and I'll—!"

"Major Pratt!"

The senior officer's word rapped out like machine-gun bullets.

"Be sensible, Pratt!" he went on. "We've got to find out about these planes. There's everything at stake."

"Yes, but don't you see, sir?" the other cut in. "If that spy told them about J Four, it stands to reason that he told them about these ships here! We'll be next. And we can't afford to lose these ships. With working drawings and everything destroyed at the

J Four factory, God knows how long it would take us to rebuild the same design if we lost these three. Why risk everything until we're sure of what we're doing?"

General Bradley stood scowling thoughtfully down at the floor. Dusty watched them intently; first one and then the other. Suddenly, he stiffened as a thought crashed home.

"Pardon, sir," he addressed the general. "I think that you're both right, and wrong."

"What the devil do you mean?" Bradley barked gruffly.

Dusty leaned forward, fighting to keep the eagerness out of his voice, and yet make it sound convincing.

"We can't delay things by bottling these ships up here, assuming that this place will withstand whatever the Blacks are doing. Yet, at the same time we can't risk running up against them in the air, yet. We don't know what the ships can do. That leaves only one thing left—one line of action. That's, put the ships where the Blacks would least expect to find them."

"And that is, where?" snapped Bradley as Dusty finished.

The pilot grinned.

"Leave that to me, sir," he said.

The other snorted wrathfully.

"How do I know where you'll take them?" he growled.

"You don't, sir," replied Dusty quietly. "But you didn't know that the assistant radio officer was a Black agent, and that he'd learned your secret, did you? Well, what I'm getting at is, that a secret is only a real secret when just one person knows it! I'll report eventually, but in the meantime—just in case—let us just carry on as before. As though it were a secret test we're making."

Both Bradley and Pratt eyed him long and hard in absolute silence. It was the former C.O. of the Dayton test field who eventually broke the silence.

He addressed his words to the senior officer.

"Ayres' plan is the best, sir," he said. "I withdraw my previous remarks. After all, there is no guarantee that the planes would be safe from destruction, even here. We don't know what the Blacks are doing. Frankly, I'm willing to stake their safe keeping on Ayres' judgment."

Dusty gave the man a look of thanks. But Pratt didn't see it. He was looking at General Bradley. A minute became two, three, and then the senior officer nodded shortly.

"Very well," he grunted, giving Dusty a keen glance. "We'll try your plan. But, remember, captain, use your best judgment. You understand?"

Dusty understood the true meaning behind the words. He simply nodded.

"Yes, sir," he said. Then to Curly and Biff, "Let's get going. Take off one at a time. Use your wing lights up to twenty thousand over the field. Then drop in behind me, and douse all lights. I'll signal directions later. Got it?"

The other two nodded, and started over toward the ramp. The wall section was being closed up. But at an order from Major Pratt it was opened again and the three sleek planes dollied up and onto level ground for the second time.

LESS THAN ten minutes later, Dusty eased open the throttle and started his take-off. Biff and Curly were already in the air. Biff's departure had almost finished in disaster. He'd opened up too quickly, and the powerful engine had snapped the ship forward like an arrow leaving a bow string. Biff's feet, obviously jerked free of the rudder pedal straps, had allowed the ship to start swinging in a crazy half-circle and go tearing straight for a line of steel and stone barracks. In the last split second, before death would have smashed him to a pulp, the big pilot had regained control, and gone thundering up into the clear.

But it had been seconds in hell for all and Dusty determined to take no chances until he had got the "feel" of his new aerial steed. Cockpit sealed, air pressure and body pressure regulator at the correct adjustment, he let the plane slide forward at half throttle, then opened up wide, easing the stick as he did so.

Taking off in the Silver Flash had always given him a big kick. The ship had seemed to virtually leap into the air from a standing start. But this new job! It was almost like the ground dropping away from you. A mighty roar of the engine—a split second's interval of blurred ground—and, presto, there was air on all sides.

Like a bullet the plane shot heavenward, and Dusty's blood danced through his veins from the sheer joy of being master of such a craft. Cowl light on, he studied the array of instruments recording the every function of the engine. At intervals he tested the controls this way and that for quickness of response. He even killed the engine, hauling back from full-out to zero, then rammed the throttle wide open again. And all the time the craft soared up toward the stars.

Not until the altimeter needle showed thirty thousand feet, did Dusty relax. Then he slouched back against the headrest, a happy grin on his face.

"Sweet essence of tripe!" he breathed fiercely. "Is this a crate, or is this a crate! Not fly one of these babies with the gang? Bradley, you may be a chief of staff, but I'm saying, nuts to you, general! We'll chin over your goofy idea, later—and how!"

With a savage nod to emphasize his remarks, Dusty waggled his wings and then sat watching as two sets of tiny lights swung in close and took up follow-the-leader positions behind him. That accomplished, he snapped off his own wing lights, flipped on radio contact and spun the wave-length dial.

"Shine kindly light every now and then, children!" he barked into the transmitter tube.

A moment later the red signal light of the panel blinked, and Curly Brooks' voice crackled in the earphones.

"Got you, papa!"

Dusty grinned and snapped off contact.

"Hope Biff got it, too," he grunted.

Whether Biff understood the true meaning—that every now and then he should flash his wing lights so that they could keep pace and direction with him in the dark sky—he did not know. Nor did he know that high above him cruel lips were pressed together in a thin line, and that equally cruel eyes burned with perplexed wonder at what their owner's ear had heard over the radio.

None of that Dusty knew. Nor did he even dream of it, as

he swung around in a half turn and set the arrow-head snout of his ship dead on for the Louisville base.

Less than an hour later he was directly over the area. Cutting throttle a bit, he started sliding down through the dark sky. But as he leaned forward and peered earthward, he saw nothing but darkness. To the four points of the compass were a strangling of lights, but, the Louisville base was like a great inky blotch in a carpet of twinkling stars.

Lower and lower he went, but every decrease in height brought the same result. The Louisville base was enshrouded with what almost seemed to be a permanent blanket of darkness.

"No soap here," he grunted, arcing heavenward again. "Can't tell until daylight. But guess I'll take a squint at J Four, just the same."

Climbing back up, he flashed his wing lights for a split second to give Biff and Curly his position, and then he goosed the 3,000 h.p. X Diesel to maximum power. Back at thirty thousand again, he flashed the follow-the-leader signal, and then set a course northwest toward J Four area, seven hundred miles away.

Three hundred of those seven hundred miles of air space had whipped past the cockpit when, suddenly, it happened!

The first notice he received was the blinking of the red signal light. Flipping up contact, he spun the dial. He had to turn it to almost zero kc. before he got any reception in the phones. And when he did, his ear-drums seemed to snap in two. His ears were affected by the volume of sound, and his heart went cold with memory of hearing it before. It was the same sing-songy sound that all three of them had heard while heading for Cleveland experimental depot in the cabin job!

PERHAPS IT was instinct born of that memory that made him cast his eyes upward. At any rate, he did, and there, miles off to his right, something was tracing a circle of faint purple sparks against the black background. Breath clamped in his lungs, he stared at the eerie phenomenon, hardly conscious that the sound blasting out of the earphones was like steel barbs piercing his ear-drums.

Then suddenly he realized that the circle of sparks was drawing nearer and nearer to a position directly above him. Like a flash he shot out his free hand, and spun the wave-length dial to the emergency reading. There was no time to waste contacting Curly and Biff in turn.

"Split!" he bellowed into the transmitter tube. "Cut out! Meet you at the spilled drink later!"

Even as he shouted the words, he slapped his ship around in a savage split arc turn, and went thundering off at right angles. Three times he repeated the maneuver until presently the ever-increasing circle of purple sparks was far off his left wings. Then, keeping his eyes glued to it, he pulled the nose up and fed his X Diesel every drop of hop it would take.

Fifteen minutes later his altimeter needle quivered at the forty-five thousand foot marker, and the circle of sparks was a good mile below him.

"Now!" he grated. "We'll see what the hell this is all about!"

Shoving the stick forward, he sent the ship racing down through the night, dead-on for the circle of sparks. Perhaps a

Biff Bolton

thousand feet had rushed past, when suddenly a voice crackled out of his earphones. It was harsh and rasping, yet there was a sort of husky undertone that that lent an even more sinister quality to the tone.

He didn't bother to analyze it in part. No sooner had he heard it than memory leaped back over the weeks—back to the night when he and Biff Bolton had been trapped by a mysterious flight of enemy ships as they were trying to sneak into C-58 area, far behind the Black lines in Canada. Then, this same voice had come to him over the radio. And now, almost forgotten, he was hearing its mysterious note again.

"Down there is death, Captain Ayres! So is there death above you! Your two swine friends are already gone—and now it is your turn. From his grave, the Black Hawk reaches up to avenge—now!"

The last was no less than a hideous scream of berserk rage. And almost instantly the entire heavens became alive with showering purple fire. It hissed, darted, and sprayed out in all directions. A million tongues of it seemed to lick out at Dusty, but none touched him, for even as he heard the first word instinct had caused him to half roll over and cut back in the opposite direction at maximum throttle. And now he was staring back over his shoulder at an eerie spectacle that made the blood run cold in his veins.

Silhouetted against the fused purple shower were a dozen phantom-like planes circling around and around in a continuous circle, one behind the other.

To see them clearly was impossible, for though the purple

shower that seemed to spew down from their bellies silhouetted their shapes, at the same time its shimmering brilliance blotted out all detail. Beyond the first circle was a second circle, perhaps three thousand feet higher. And above them a small dark moving blur, the sight of which pulled Dusty's eyelids down to narrowed slits.

"You're the one who interests me most, sweetheart!" he grated. "I'm thinking you're the head man of this show. We'll see, anyway!"

Engine at only three-quarter throttle, he climbed slowly up, making sure to keep well clear of the eerie purple phenomena. The small moving blur was less than three hundred yards off his left and about five hundred feet below, when he finally leveled off and swung around, nose to it. Even at that distance it was only a moving blur. But that fact did not worry him. Time to get a good look, just before he opened fire.

"Now bum!" he grated shoving the nose down. "Let's play it my way!"

But hardly had the last word ripped off his lips, than something happened that left him cursing at himself.

THE TWO circles of purple sparks blinked out, and instantly the entire heavens became a void of inky soup. Reason for the action came to Dusty at once. He had not switched off transmission, and every word he had been grating to himself had gone zipping out over the ether waves. Hell, he might just as well have written his mysterious and unknown foe a letter of what he intended to do.

Mentally kicking himself, he pulled out of his dive, and went wing-screaming upward. Part of him, burning with chagrin at his own thoughtless stupidity, urged him to go down and hunt them out in the dark. But the other part of him, the cold, sane reasoning part, argued against such a maneuver, and won.

There was little to gain, and much to lose. He stood one chance of lining up a target in the darkness, as against a million chances of handing himself a fare-thee-well mid-air crash. And besides, Curly and Biff might still be around, and he couldn't risk—

The unfinished thought jerked him up with a start. God, yes, Curly and Biff! Had they understood his guarded order, and high-balled back to Group Seven's field—back to the spilled drink?

Perhaps Biff, yes. But it was doubtful about Curly. It would take more than an order to get that crazy Indian away from this weird set-up. Most likely he was floating around somewhere. Or had he—Dusty's heart went stone cold—had Curly or Biff been caught in that purple shower, whatever the hell it was?

Dusty battled with the nerve-jangling thought for a moment or two, then cursed and spun the wave-length dial to the emergency reading. As he grabbed up the transmitter tube he peered out into the night-flooded heavens.

"Buzzards!" he yelled. "On deck?"

Thirty seconds of hell dragged by in utter silence. Then he repeated the call. Thirty seconds more and then the signal light blinked. The voice that crackled out of the earphones belonged to Biff Bolton.

"On deck, skipper!"

"Seen any beanpoles?" snapped Dusty in a guarded tone.

"Huh?" came back the startled ejaculation.

"A beanpole with curls!" said Dusty.

A long moment of silence. Then out of the earphones:

"Was near one once. It fell away, suddenly. Don't know why or how."

The last was like a knife twisting in Dusty's heart. He tried to make himself believe that Curly had already landed at Seven's drome. But a sane bit of calculation made that out an impossibility, instantly. In the time allowed, Curly couldn't have made Seven's drome, even in the ship he was flying.

A faint groan welled up from Dusty's throat, and he tossed all caution to the four winds.

"Curly! Curly Brooks!" he thundered into the transmitter tube. "Two-Four-Two calling! Check-back to Two-Four-Two!"

Five, ten, fifteen seconds of heart-torturing silence dragged by into oblivion. But not even a whisper of Curly's voice came out of the air. Dusty cursed and bellowed into the transmitter tube. It only made his throat dry and his lungs ache.

And then out of the great limitless void of pitch darkness came the harsh, rasping, and huskily undertoned voice of the mysterious pilot.

"My condolences, Captain Ayres. But your friend is but one of millions who is doomed. It has been so pledged!"

The English-spoken words were followed by some Black Invader jargon that Dusty did not understand or try to. And then the red light blinked out and the radio clicked into silence.

CHAPTER 4
BLACK CHALLENGE

FOR A long moment Dusty sat peering out at the darkened skies, hoping against hope to see even a tiny flicker of exhaust flame that would give him a clue as to the position of his unknown enemy. But he saw nothing; absolutely nothing. He might just as well be flying around in a plate of thick soup.

He thought of Biff Bolton somewhere out there in space. And with that thought came reluctant decision. Spinning the wave-length dial to the emergency reading, he bent over the transmitter tube.

"Back to the spilled drink, Biff!" he snapped.

The order off his chest, he pulled the nose up and gave the ship its head. Twenty thousand feet higher he leveled off and risked a flash of the cowl light to check compass direction. Then, with eyes straining out into the darkness, he set an as-the-crow-flies course for the drome of H.S. Group Seven, just outside Springfield, Mass.

Two hours later he was sliding down toward it, prop just ticking over and heart thumping against his ribs in eerie dread. So silent had been his approach that his wheels were almost touching before the floodlights snapped on. Wheel-breaking slightly, once he touched rubber, he taxied around and up to an end hangar. In the dull glow of tarmac lights he saw Biff Bolton come running out to him. The big pilot jumped up on the fuselage step and bellowed through the orange-peel glass cockpit cowl.

"Taxi her right inside, skipper! Mine's in there. And there's plenty of room!"

Dusty grinned his admiration. Bolton had used his head, alright. No sense in leaving secret designs out in the open for unwanted eyes to get a look at.

Two minutes later he had killed his engine and was legging out as mechanics rolled the heavy doors closed.

"Curly?" he snapped at Biff. "He here too?"

The big pilot shook his head.

"Nope," he said. "Maybe he's on his way. But—"

Dusty's heart skipped a beat as the other faltered.

"But what?" he demanded.

Bolton seemed reluctant to speak.

"That purple stuff," he said in a hesitating tone. "I lost him in it. He was spinning at the time. Didn't see him again. God, skipper, what do you suppose it was?"

Before Dusty could answer, the small door in the big right hand sliding door opened, and Major Drake came briskly inside. He gave the two planes a flashing glance of frank approval then fastened his eyes on Dusty.

"What's all this about, Ayres?" he asked. "Just got back from an H.Q. chin-fest. Where's Brooks?"

"We don't know, sir," the pilot answered. "He—"

He cut off the rest, flicked his eyes about the interior of the hangar.

"I think we'd better talk in your office, major," he said. "Will you please give orders to mount guard on this hangar? A double guard it had better be. No one is to enter—not even any of the gang. And have the officer in charge of the field's detector units keep his ears open, too. At the slightest warning, we're clearing out."

The C.O. arched his eyebrows and looked puzzled.

"Bad as that?" he grunted. Dusty nodded absently. He was thinking of Curly.

"Worse, I'm afraid," he said slowly.

"Hell, and I thought I was being smart!"

Major Drake made no comment. He turned and led the way out of the hangar. After issuing the necessary orders he led them over to the field office. Once inside he turned to Dusty.

"Now, let's have the whole thing from beginning to end," he demanded.

Dusty took a deep breath, and then related his experiences in detail.

"Perhaps the ships would have been safe if we'd left them at Cleveland," he finished up. "But—well, I dreaded what General Bradley might decide to do with me next. Also, it struck me as a smart trick to sneak the ships right up here—right under the Blacks' noses where they'd least expect to find them. In that I pulled a boner. Don't know for sure, but I'm betting that some Black saw our take-off. And, of course, my flashing wing-lights every now and then—another trick I thought was smart—made it simple for them to follow us. Curly gone—somewhere. God, what a blasted mess I've made of it all!"

HEAVY SILENCE settled over the office as Dusty stopped talking. Eyes glazed with bitterness and rage at self as he stared unseeing at the floor. The other two looked at him, faces expressionless. Presently Major Drake shook his head from side to side.

"It's hard to say whether you did right or wrong," he said quietly. "As you mentioned, not knowing what the devil this new thing is that the Blacks have, keeping the planes at Cleveland was no guarantee of safety. Particularly, when it's quite evident that the Blacks knew that they were there. As regards General Bradley's new idea—well, there might be a better way of getting around that than taking the reins in your own hands."

"Yes, I realize that," said Dusty dully. "But, dammit, the very thought of a blasted swivel chair job just seemed to make something inside of me blow up. My place is in a cockpit—and, by God, that's where I'm going to stick."

Knowing his ace pilot from A to Z, Major Drake didn't make the foolish mistake of clouding up and raining all over him with flowery words of devotion to duty, no matter what that duty might be, and so forth. He simply nodded his head in perfect understanding of the pilot's inner feelings.

"Well," he said. "You haven't actually been ordered to Washington as yet. And a lot of things can happen in a very short time. But forgetting that angle for the moment—what's your explanation of those purple sparks you saw and the ships in circle formation?"

Dusty frowned; bit his lower lip.

"No explanation," he said. "Couldn't see the damn things clearly. That one ship I started to attack seemed to be of a different type from the others. The pilot was the fleet leader, I guess."

He turned to Bolton.

"Can you add anything, Biff?" he asked.

The big pilot ran a thumb nail down the side of his jaw and glanced meditatively at the opposite wall.

"Well," he drawled. "Yes, and no. Don't know just how to put it—maybe I'm crazy."

"Let's hear it anyway, Bolton," Major Drake cut in impatiently.

"Yes, sir. Well, just after the skipper, here, told us to light out, something went down past me, hell-bent for election. A ship, of course—but the damnedest looking thing I ever saw. Seemed to me all wing, and a mighty small one at that. But of course it was dark and I couldn't see for sure. Anyway, the next thing I knew, the sky's all purple-like. And Brooks was spinning down, power on. I started to follow him, when suddenly, I thought my ship was on fire. It was so hot that for a second I thought I was cooked. So help me, but I'll swear that the power generator on the radio actually started to smoke. And the next thing I knew I'm upside down, everything is pitch dark and your on-deck question, skipper, is clicking in my earphones. From then on until I sat down on this field I didn't see or hear a damn thing."

Dusty's heart stood still as he asked the question.

"Was Curly's ship on fire? Do—do you think that he was dead?"

Bolton shrugged.

"It wasn't on fire," he said with decided conviction. Then in a lower voice, "The last—I don't know. He went down too fast for me to get a good look."

With a part moan, part curse, Dusty got to his feet and started pacing restlessly up and down the length of the office. Major Drake allowed him to work off some of his emotional steam, then reached out and grabbed his arm.

"Sit down," he said quietly but firmly. "Brooks has disappeared before and come up O.K. And, either way, he'd be the last to want us to sit around and just mope over him. There's work for us to do."

Dusty flung himself into a chair.

"You're dead right, sir," he sighed heavily. "What's the next move?"

The C.O. pulled a letter from his tunic pocket and held it out.

"First you can open this," he said. "It's addressed to you. Corporal Carter found it in a message dropper on the drome early this evening."

"Message dropper?" echoed Dusty, taking the letter. "Dropped by air? Didn't the detectors pick up the ship's engine?"

"They did," nodded the C.O. "But it was an American engine. It is not the first time that the Blacks have used American engines to fool our detector units."

Dusty made no comment. He ripped open the envelope, pulled out the sheet of paper inside and glanced at the pen-scrawled words.

To Captain Ayres:

THE BLACK AVENGER

He who was the greatest of us all has been killed by your hand. We, the living, have pledged to avenge our loss a thousandfold. Within twenty-four hours you and your dog comrades will be wiped from the face of the earth. Nothing can save you. YOU ARE DOOMED!

Ekar,

The Avenger.

Dusty read it through twice, then stared hard at the signature.

"Ekar?" he echoed aloud. "What in hell is that? Sounds like a new kind of breakfast food to me. Now who in—?"

The rest was drowned out by the loud jangle of the deskphone bell. He scooped up the instrument, announced his presence, then stiffened as he heard the excited voice of Agent 10 at the other end of the wire.

"Ayres! Ayres! Abandon your field at once. Get out, all of you! The Blacks have something that can annihilate anything. Get out, man! Get out fast!"

"Wait, listen!" shouted Dusty as the other seemed to ring off. "Where are you? I've got to see you! There's something important that—"

Suddenly there was a moan of pain at the other end of the wire. An instant later it was followed by a dull thud as though some heavy object had fallen to the floor.

Dusty squeezed the instrument so tightly that his knuckles showed white under the skin.

"Jack! Jack! What's up—what's up?"

Silence for several seconds. Then a low moan—and a voice. It was no more than a hoarse whisper.

"Get out—at once! Blacks have—NF—NF—eight—"

The rest trailed off into a low, drawn out sigh. Dusty pounded his free fist on the desk.

"Jack! Where are you—where are you?"

The only answer he received was the sharp click of the instrument as contact was shut off. He cursed and jiggled the contact lever up and down.

"Corps exchange!" he bellowed. "Corps exchange! Where did that call for Seventh Group come from? Snap it up! Emergency!"

"Yes, sir," a voice clipped out. "Just a minute."

A hellish wait of several seconds, then the voice spoke again.

"Relayed by radio-phone from Washington Signal H.Q., sir. Transmitted via Galveston to check against listening in. Can I help you further, sir?"

"No, thanks," said Dusty, and slapped the phone back into its cradle.

"What the—"

Dusty silenced Major Drake's question with a quick motion of his hand. And in a few rapid-fire sentences he spoke of the conversation.

"It was Jack Horner, all right," he said. "I couldn't possibly mistake his voice. NF-Eight? That's southeastern Newfoundland. But Jack's call came through from Washington Signal H.Q."

He stopped short and frowned down at the letter that both Drake and Biff Bolton had already read. Then he glanced up quickly at the C.O.

"I suggest we take the tip, sir, and clear out," he said bluntly.

Drake's shoulders went back and his square chin jutted out.

"Damned if I'll let those rats' threats put me on the run!" he grated.

Dusty leaned forward.

"Maybe, sir," he said pointedly, "whether or not they threatened Louisville Base and J Four I don't know. But I do know they made good. Until we track this thing down to its source we can't afford to take foolish risks. My bet is for the whole group to move, and in the meantime I'll get to work—somehow."

"You'll get to work?" echoed the other sharply. Then in even sharper tone, "just what is on your mind?"

"Washington Signal H.Q. first," Dusty answered right back. "I've got to find out what happened to Agent 10. Then I'll begin from there."

Major Drake was far from impressed.

"And if Agent 10 has been killed?" he said meaningly.

Dusty swallowed hard. Curly and Jack Horner? God—!

"I'm hoping against that," he said lamely. "But dammit, I've got to do something, can't just sit around and wait for things to happen. Maybe General Horner knows something. I'll see him. Hell, I'll do anything except this blasted walking around in the dark!"

He cut off the rest abruptly and snatched up the mysterious warning.

"Ekar!" he grated. "The avenger, eh? Well, we'll see about that!"

"Hold it, Ayres!" Drake's voice drowned out his words. "Now

hold your horses! We'll go at this thing right. Washington Signal H.Q., eh? Well, we'll see. Step aside a minute."

Brushing past Dusty, the Group C.O. went around in back of the desk and sat down. Shooting out a hand he snapped on the portable short wave set, and spun the wave-length dial. Then he bent toward the built-in transmitter unit.

"Calling Washington air force H.Q. Emergency on wave-length Four-Five! Other stations clear air for this call please. Major Drake, Seven! Calling Washington air force H.Q."

The fingers of his free hand drumming absently on the desktop, the C.O. sat otherwise perfectly still, eyes glued on the red signal light. One, two, three minutes dragged by, but the light did not blink.

He repeated his call, and waited again. Still no answer. Cursing softly he spun the wave-length dial to a different wave-length reading. And again nothing but silence. He was just in the act of trying a third wave-length when suddenly the office door burst open and Williams, officer in charge of the field's main station, came bounding inside. His face was white as a sheet and his voice trembled as he spoke.

"Major! Major," he gasped out. "Something's wrong! Something must be wrong! I can't raise a single station—or get anything! Every wave-length is being static jammed! We're absolutely cut off!"

CHAPTER 5
AGENT 10

BEFORE ANYONE had a chance to make any comment, Dusty leaped for the desk, grabbed up the ground phone, and jiggled the contact hook up and down.

"Corps exchange!" he shouted. "Get me through to Washington H.Q. at once! Get me through to—"

He didn't finish, for it was then that he became conscious of a jangling sort of buzzing sound in the receiver. Past experience told him instantly that he was shouting into the sound oscillations of an over-revving power generator. In other words, the ground wire had also gone haywire. Slowly he put the instrument back in its cradle, looked at Major Drake.

"I suggest we abandon the field, sir," he said in a steady voice. "We'd be fools to stick it out and call their bluff. I don't believe it's a bluff this time."

Major Drake scowled hard at the floor, and balled his fingers into sledge hammer fists. Presently he nodded his head abruptly.

"Perhaps you're right," he grunted. "For the time being we'll move to Twenty's field at Albany. But, you, Ayres? You're—"

"A favor, sir," Dusty cut in. "As far as you know, I haven't been here since I first left for Cleveland with Brooks and Bolton."

The C.O. gave him a long piercing look, then shrugged.

"Very well," he said, "we'll leave like that—for the present. You want leave before I route the others out?"

Dusty grinned.

"If you don't mind," he said, turning toward the door. "I'll try and contact you at Albany, later."

With a quick salute, Dusty ducked outside. He had not missed the pleading look in Biff Bolton's eyes, but he had purposely ignored the big pilot. For the present, it was best for Biff to lend his aid in evacuating the field. Right now, Dusty wanted to be alone. Too many mysterious things had piled up for him to take on the additional responsibility of a flying mate.

In swift strides he went over to the hangar line, took the guard's salute and issued orders for his new ship to be dollied out. Five minutes later he went streaking across the night-shadowed field and pulled up into the black sky. All lights out, he climbed until twenty thousand feet of air space was beneath his wing. Then leveling off, he snapped on radio contact and spun the wave-length dial.

"Calling Washington air force H.Q.!" he shouted into the transmitter tube. "Group Seven abandoning present field moving to N.H. Five! Captain Ayres calling and proceeding to that location."

Three times he repeated the call, purposely ignoring the blinking of the red signal light that indicated that Washington air force H.Q. was trying to check back.

"Or maybe it's you, Bradley," he grunted. "Sorry, but the receiving end of my set isn't working for the moment!"

With a nod for emphasis, he abruptly changed his course and headed full-out, straight for the nation's capital. He was less than a hundred miles north of it when, suddenly, the red signal light began to blink again. He glanced at the dial, noted that some station was trying to contact on his own emergency wave-length, and stiffened in the seat. The call was coming-in over two-four-two—the wave-length that he and Curly Brooks had long ago agreed to use only in case of vital emergency. Curly—Curly was trying to contact him!

His free hand flew out like a flash and snapped on contact, then grabbed up the transmitter tube.

"Kid!" he exclaimed. "Where are you?"

But no sound came from the earphones.

"Two-four-two!" he shouted anew. "Two-four-two! Check with me at once!"

BUT STILL there was no answer in the earphones. At intervals of two minutes he repeated his plea. But for all the good it did him, he might just as well be calling to a brick wall. Yet the eerie part of it was—the red signal light continued to blink! Some station was on his wave-length. If not that, then his set had suddenly gone completely haywire.

The last he proved not to be the case by a careful scrutiny of the recording dials. The dials could not lie. Everything was in perfect working order. Yet, even as the lights of Washington seeped up over the southern horizon, the earphones were still silent.

And then, as though the whole thing had been perfectly timed—timed right to the instant he eased back the throttle and started down toward the military field—a voice crackled out of the earphones. It was a voice harsh and rasping, with a husky undertone.

"Thank you, Captain Ayres," it said. "Since I lost you at Louisville I have been trying hard to make contact again."

As Dusty gulped in utter amazement the red signal light blinked out and the radio set went silent.

"What the hell? It's that tramp again!"

Dusty's words echoed back and jerked him out of his befuddled trance. Ramming on power he zoomed up and circled about, striving desperately to pierce the blanket of darkness that enshrouded both heaven and earth. But it was all just a waste of time, and fuel.

Finally, burning with baffled rage, he jammed the stick forward and sent the plane thundering down toward the Washington military field. Floodlights greeted his landing, and a couple of greaseballs ran forward as he taxied up, killed his engine and legged out. One of them, a corporal, recognized him immediately. He saluted smartly.

"You, skipper?" he gasped. "We heard that you got yours at Cleveland Experimental. It—"

"What's that!" Dusty yelled. "Cleveland Experimental? Anything happened?"

The other nodded.

"And how!" he exclaimed. "The field station, here, picked up the S.O.S.—wiped, right clean off the map, so they say. Nothing left."

Dusty flinched, started to shoot more questions at the noncom, then changed his mind.

"Corporal!" he snapped instead. "Watch this ship. My orders—plug anyone who comes within fifty yards of it! Anyone, understand? I'll be back later."

Leaving the two greaseballs gaping after him, he spun around and raced toward the motor park at the end of the hangar line. A sergeant in charge saluted him as he approached.

"Yes, sir?" he started.

But Dusty didn't even check his pace. He tore past the man,

leaped into the nearest car and slid behind the wheel. The sergeant shouted something, but it was lost in the roar of the car's engine as Dusty banged down on the starter and pressed the electro gear mesh button in practically the same movement.

Like a shell leaving the bore of a naval gun, the car leaped into high speed from a standing start and shot across the field. An attack plane was taking off on the floodlighted runway, and for a second Dusty's heart stood still. But not his muscles. With all his might he pulled the wheel down hard to the right.

Rubber screamed and a shower of dirt and small stone spewed backward. Then hard down to the left he pulled the wheel. A terrific blast of prop-wash struck him broadside, as he tore past the tail of the ship. And then he was tearing across even ground again, little beads of cold sweat trickling down off his forehead.

The far side of the field sloped up to the main highway. He took the slope at half speed, slued around onto the highway facing Washington. Then, with the side button jammed down and locked, he gave the thirty-two small bore cylinders under the hood everything they could take.

In front of him midnight traffic and pedestrians, most of them in uniform, scurried frantically to the left and right. And behind him half a dozen police and military motor patrols gave furious chase. But when he finally brake-slammed into the curb in front of Signal H.Q., just across the broad avenue from the War Department building, they were all far back in his dust.

In exactly ten strides he went up the thirty stone steps and charged in through the wide swinging doors. A startled major seated behind a desk, leaped up.

"Here!" he demanded. "What the devil?"

Dusty didn't even bother to salute. He simply grabbed the officer.

"Lieutenant Horner!" he barked. "He called me from your main exchange room. Something happened to him. Where—?"

"Wait, wait, hold it!" the other cut him off. "You're Ayres, aren't you? Yes, he was asking for you. That's all we could get out of him—just your name. The rest was all garbled up."

"What happened?" Dusty asked. "And where is he now?"

The senior officer seemed to be glad of an audience. He took a deep breath.

"Well, it was like this," he began. "The lieutenant asked me for phone connections to some unit via Galveston. Very important he said. As a matter of fact, he looked quite flustered. Something bothered him no doubt."

"Yes, yes?" fumed Dusty, as the other paused to take another deep breath. "But what happened?"

The major frowned.

"I'm coming to that!" he said irritably. "Anyway, I sent him to Exchange Four room—sixteenth floor. He was there quite a spell. It made me wonder. I called main exchange, and found that he'd finished his call. So I sent an orderly corporal up there. Well, it certainly gave me a shock, I can tell you. Right here in Washington! Can you imagine it?"

"Imagine what?" Dusty fairly bellowed. "What happened?"

"A mystery if there ever was one!" nodded the other emphatically. "The knife must have been used with tremendous force. It's a miracle if it didn't pierce his heart. He's at the naval hospital now—closest one, you know. But I certainly can't understand how—here, where are you going I haven't—"

BUT DUSTY was already through the swinging doors and bounding down the stone steps. At least a dozen cars, police and military, were parked about his. A couple of dozen voices started to bellow questions. He grabbed a police lieutenant whose car was out of the jam.

"Important!" he rapped out, dragging the man across the street. "The naval hospital at once. Emergency. Life or death! Let's go!"

Perhaps the police lieutenant recognized Dusty, or perhaps he was one of the rare few who act and ask questions later. At any rate, without a word he leaped into his car, paused long enough for Dusty to swing in beside him, and then sent the car rocketing down the wide avenue.

Dusty had driven to Signal H.Q. at top speed, but it was a snail's pace compared to the speed at which the police lieutenant sent his car across the city. In fact, hardly had Dusty flung himself back against the cushions before the driver swung his car into the half moon driveway of the naval hospital and skidded to a stop.

"Thanks," said Dusty, and went over the side without bothering to open the door.

In the hospital lobby he immediately buttonholed the officer in charge of the floor.

"Lieutenant Horner," he said. "Where is he?"

"Room seven, third ward, twelfth floor," was the instant answer. "Who are you?"

Dusty introduced himself, started to ask the other to take him up, when the officer cut in.

"Understand he was asking for you, captain. Come along."

Turning abruptly on his heel the officer led the way over to the elevator row. An express car took them aloft in nothing flat. And as Dusty stepped off, the first person he saw was General Horner, chief of Intelligence.

The big man's eyes widened with surprise as he saw Dusty. Then he hurried over to him.

"Ayres!" he boomed. "Good God—I heard you were killed. What the devil are you doing here?"

Dusty ignored the last question and asked the one uppermost in his mind.

"How is he, sir?"

The senior officer's face went grave, and he visibly clamped down on his obviously jangled nerves.

"Don't know," he said. "He's coming out of the ether now. The knife broke and they had to operate. The surgeons are with him now."

Dusty could feel little fingers of ice clutching at his heart. He swallowed hard and forced himself to keep his voice calm.

"What exactly happened, sir?" he asked.

The other pursed his lips in frowning thought.

"No one seems to know," he said at length. "The first word I got was when they brought him here. I didn't even know he was in the city. Believed him to be any place, except here. He was making a code phone call from Signal H.Q., they tell me. Then he was found in the sealed room with a knife in his chest.

Who, what, or how—I don't know. But they tell me that he's been saying your name."

Dusty nodded, and told the general of the call he had received. The senior officer went a shade or two paler. For a long moment he didn't speak. He simply stood rigid, staring hard at a door upon which was the number, seven. Presently, a long drawn out sigh slid off his lips, and he looked at Dusty again.

"There's the devil to pay all along the line, Ayres," he said gruffly. "Those rats have got something this time. Something that beats anything else they've tried so far. If we can't find it out and block them—heaven help us. But how is it that you're still alive? I heard that you were killed at Cleveland."

In a few clipped-off sentences, Dusty told his story. The general listened in heavy silence, which he prolonged even after Dusty had finished.

"A damned mixed-up mess if there ever was one!" he suddenly got out savagely. "Some one has taken the Black Hawk's place, that's evident."

"And he seems to be twice as clever as the Hawk was," added Dusty grimly. "He tricked me into giving away my position, neat as could be. Used my secret wave-length call, and—hell yes, I'm a dope! He undoubtedly heard me calling Curly on that wave-length when I was trying to locate him. Then, when I was trying to raise a check-back on what I thought was a call from Curly, he simply kept his mouth shut, and spotted my position on his directional finder dial. Damn him—he is clever!"

GENERAL HORNER'S eyes had wandered back to the door of room 7 again. Dusty looked at it also, and absently guessed that the same thought was in both their minds. A clue, if any, to the horrible mystery was in the brain of the Intelligence man lying dangerously wounded behind that closed door. If he died, their hopes might die with him.

Minutes, long, soul-torturing minutes dragged by. The officer who had brought Dusty up in the elevator attempted to make conversation. But neither Dusty nor General Horner even attempted to listen to him, and he finally lapsed into silence.

A quarter of an hour, a half—and then the door of room 7 opened, and a man in white came out into the corridor and walked toward them. Dusty looked at the other's face. It was grave, almost expressionless. He stopped in front of General Horner, looked him square in the eye.

The senior officer's shoulders went back.

"Well?" he said in a strained voice.

"I'm unable to tell at the moment, general," the medical surgeon replied. "Right now I might give him a fifty-fifty chance to pull through. The left lung was grazed. If the tissue holds, and there is no internal hemorrhage—he has a chance. But—"

The man paused. General Horner held him with his eyes.

"But what?" he rapped out tersely.

The medical surgeon gestured slightly.

"He does not seem to want that chance, sir," he said. "He can just barely talk. Insists upon seeing you—or a Captain Ayres. Says it's of vital importance. But he refuses bluntly to give me an inkling of what it's all about. Frankly, he seems more perturbed about some secret on his mind than the matter of his life."

General Horner stood still as marble.

"And if he should talk to me?" he asked with an effort.

"I couldn't possibly hold out hope, sir," replied the other. "Talking would wear down completely what little resistance he now has. True, I might be wrong. We doctors are not infallible, and miracles have happened. But, in this case—"

The medical officer finished it with a shrug, and nervously shifted his weight from one foot to the other. Dusty wanted to look at General Horner, but he couldn't bring himself to do it. He could only picture the hellish torture that must be his.

Behind the door of room 7 lay his only son, wavering between life and death. But it was obvious that he possessed information of untold value. In his brain, perhaps, was the key clue to the hellish devastation that was swirling down upon the United States. For General Horner to learn that secret, and be in a position to act, might mean the life of his son. But to wait until Jack Horner's thread of life had been strengthened might mean—Suddenly Dusty was conscious of a hand on his shoulder. He half turned, met the strained eyes of General Horner. The senior officer's lips moved and words came from between them as though they had been dragged up from the very soles of his boots.

"Come along, Ayres. We've got to find out."

Just those few words, nothing more. But in the mere saying of them, the Intelligence chief had put behind him the one thing in life nearest and dearest to him. Put it behind him for something even greater—flag and country.

Dusty nodded. And together they started toward the door of room 7.

CHAPTER 6
SPINNING HELL

A GRADUATE nurse, trim, neat and efficient-looking was sitting beside the bed as Dusty and General Horner came into the room. She looked up, frowned slightly, made a slight silencing gesture. Dusty glanced at the form under the covers.

Jack Horner was lying on his left side. His face was deathly pale even through the heavy tan, and his eyes were closed. For one horrible moment Dusty thought that his pal was dead—he was so still, so utterly motionless. Then the covers moved, and the blue-white lips gave forth a moan.

"Ayres—abandon your drome—get out! Ayres!—where is Ayres? He can—he must—we've got to—NF-Eight!"

Over and over again the wounded man repeated the words. Dusty was filled with a sudden desire to step closer to the bed, to call out to his friend. But something stopped him. Perhaps it was the nurse's eyes, which had gone brittle, fixed steadily upon him. At any rate, he didn't move.

And then without warning, Agent 10's eyes fluttered open. They roamed about glassily for a moment, became fixed on General Horner and Dusty, and lighted up with recognition.

"You?" faintly. "Thank God! Listen—"

It was more than Dusty could stand. He went close.

"Easy, Jack," he said gently. "Better not talk. The medico said—"

Jack Horner poured the words off his lips.

"Damn the medico! He doesn't know his ankle from a three dollar hat! I'm all right. Listen to me, both of you. The Blacks—"

He suddenly stopped, made as though to roll over on his back, and winced from the pain. Dusty put out a protesting hand. Jack Horner glared.

"That nurse—here? Get her out. You two, alone. Get her out!"

Dusty looked first at the nurse, then at General Horner. The Intelligence chief's face was almost as white as his son's.

"Leave us, nurse, please," he said in a low voice.

The nurse hesitated, cast an anxious glance at young Horner. And then without a word she went out and closed the door behind her. As it clicked shut, Jack Horner grunted.

"Much better," he said in his whispery voice. "Too damn much fuss over me. Not going to kick in—the blockheads! Listen, Ayres—you know NF-Eight?"

Dusty nodded, and the other went on.

"On the coast—northeast coast. A bit north of Shoal Harbor. It's a receiving depot for Black equipment, troops and stuff from their depots in Europe. Heavily guarded—land, water, air. But—it's there at NF-Eight. That's where the thing is."

As though the effort had been too much, Agent 10's voice trailed off and his eyes fluttered closed again. A million questions hovered on the tip of Dusty's tongue, but he didn't speak them. He probably couldn't have if he'd wanted to. The sight of Jack Horner doggedly fighting his own grim battle seemed to paralyze both mind and body.

With General Horner at his side, Dusty waited, hoping

against hope. The very silence of the room seemed to crush down upon him with terrific force. And he was about to summon the nurse when young Horner's eyes opened again.

"Where was I? Oh yes—NF-Eight, Dusty! The stuff is there—and so is Fire-Eyes. I saw him. I almost got within reach of him. We must stop it—stop it! I saw—just came back! It'll wipe us out—wipe out the whole country!"

General Horner risked a question.

"What is it, son?" he put it gently. "What have they got? What will wipe us out?"

Eyes that had suddenly gone a trifle glassy stared up at the Intelligence chief. Then young Horner's lips moved.

"Just got back—must warn Ayres—Ekar—he's a devil. Used ground wire—via Galveston—much safer! Saw that rat—he'd trailed me. Shouldn't have taken chances. Quick as a cat with that knife—seen others like him. Damn—can't hold this blasted phone! Ayres—Ekar—NF-Eight—it's there—Fire-Eyes, too! Quick—they'll wipe us out. I heard them—heard—say—your—drome! Revenge—Hawk! Abandon—abandon—abandon—"

As the voice trailed off into a faint moan, Dusty whirled for the door. General Horner did the same thing. But, as they reached the door together, it opened and the medical surgeon came in. He didn't even look at them. He went straight to the bed, bent over the still form. Behind, like a white shadow, followed the nurse. Whatever they did was shielded by their bodies. But presently the medical officer straightened up and turned. With a jerk of his head he motioned Dusty and General

Horner out into the corridor. There he spoke to the Intelligence chief.

"The best thing for him, general," he said. "A fatigue coma. I've given him something that'll keep him asleep. Anything that he might say now would simply be delirious raving. Wouldn't know what he was saying. I'll keep you posted—you'll be at your office?"

General Horner nodded like a man in a daze.

"Yes," he mumbled. "Yes, I'll be there. But—do you think— is he—I mean…."

"I won't know for another ten hours," the medico broke in. "I warned you, you know. But he seems to have the resistance of a dozen men. It'll take at least ten hours before we'll know anything—definitely."

"Ten hours," repeated the general, as though the words were some lesson that he had learned by heart. "Ten hours. Thank you, major. Keep in touch with me. Let me know instantly, if—"

"Yes, general, I will," said the medical surgeon and lead the way toward the elevators.

FROM THE moment the elevator doors closed upon them until they were both in Horner's private office in the War Department Building, neither Dusty nor the Intelligence chief spoke a single word. Going over behind his massive desk, the general dropped heavily into the chair, put his clenched fists to his temples, then lowered them and looked at Dusty.

"Maybe you think my heart's stone, Ayres!" he said gruffly, pressing his clenched fists against the desk-top. "But I'd sacrifice everything I have to beat these devils. And sacrifice it a thousand times over! They must not win!"

"Don't worry, they won't!" replied Dusty evenly. "And, if it had been my son—I'd have done the same thing. But we can't go back on him, sir. He'd never forgive us when he gets well. And he is going to get well. Jack's tough. He'll pull through. And we can't go back on him."

The senior officer looked puzzled.

"How do you mean, can't go back on him?"

Dusty leaned forward.

"We've got to finish what he started, sir," he said. "Jack found out something—found out about this thing the Blacks have that smeared Louisville, J Four factories, and Cleveland. It starts from NF-Eight. That much of what he said, I did understand. It comes to NF-Eight from Europe. And from there—down to us."

"Granted," nodded Horner. "I got that much, myself. But, what—what comes from Europe and then down here? If we only knew, then we could do something to stop it!"

"And we don't know," put in Dusty. "So our first job is to find out."

"How?"

The single word came out like a rifle bullet. Dusty didn't reply immediately. He sat gazing meditatively at the top of the desk. Finally, he looked up.

"Frankly, I can think of only one way, sir," he said. "That puts it up to me. At the field, I have the fastest thing on wings. I know the entire NF area quite well. Been there before, if you'll remember. Well, I'll go there again—and hope that my lucky star will stay with me."

General Horner was far from impressed and the look on his face showed it.

"You heard what Agent 10 said?" he grunted. "The place is guarded by land, sea, and air. What chance do you think you'll have of even getting in there, let alone finding out anything?"

Dusty shrugged.

"And what alternative do you suggest?" he asked.

The other spread his hands wide.

"The North Atlantic Battle Fleet for one," he said. "And a dozen Tetalyne bombing groups for another. We'll smash in and return their blasted wiping out compliment!"

"And while you're doing that, sir?" said Dusty, quietly. "The needle in the haystack, that we're really looking for, will be whisked off somewhere else—some other place that we don't know! I grant that your idea is good, once we know what we're looking for. But first we've got to find out just what it is. And besides, you know as well as I do that storming the NF area would be no small task."

The Intelligence chief scowled at the desk some more.

"Perhaps you're right," he rumbled. "It would take a while to concentrate the combined forces. Still, it's just as ridiculous for you to tackle the thing alone. You don't know what you may—"

He didn't finish the rest. At that instant the bell of his private phone jangled harshly. A conglomeration of expressions flitted over his moon face as he shot out his nearest hand for the instrument.

"Horner speaking!" he boomed.

Then he stiffened, bent further over the desk.

"What's that? You did. Didn't even know you were there. Eh? Heard from Ayres? Yes, right here in my office now. What? Yes, surely. We'll be here. We'll be waiting. 'Bye."

The general hung up, and looked at Dusty.

"That was Bradley," he said. "Just flew in. Missed the Cleveland catastrophe by less than fifteen minutes. Major Trapp is with him. Been trying to contact you for hours. On his way over now."

Dusty said nothing. But he thought plenty, and none of it was pleasant. In the excitement of the last couple of hours, he'd practically forgotten all about the chief of air force staff. On sudden impulse he leaned toward General Horner and told him of Bradley's plan to install him on air force staff.

"I don't want to shirk my duty handed to me, sir," he finished up. "No matter what it may be. But, hell—I'd go nuts, sir. I wouldn't be worth a damn. I wish I could make them realize that. I'm just a pilot, and—and that's all I want to be, for the present!"

General Horner made no comment, and for a moment Dusty thought that he hadn't even listened to him. He started to speak but the other raised his hand.

"Hold it—a thought just came to me."

Dusty relaxed as much as he could and sat watching the chief of Intelligence sitting there drumming the fingers of one hand on the desk, and staring unseeing off into space. Then suddenly, the big man slapped the desk and caught Dusty's eye.

"Ekar!" he cried. "By God, I thought that sounded familiar."

The exclamation, totally unexpected, sent a wild thrill shooting through Dusty. He started to speak, but checked himself. Horner had snapped on the inter-office speaker unit and was bending toward the built-in transmitter.

"Bring file B.I.-Two in here at once!" he snapped.

IT DIDN'T seem that he'd even finished talking when a side door of the room popped open, and an orderly sergeant entered. Under his arm he carried an eight-by-eleven file folder. He put it on the desk in front of the general, saluted and beat a hasty retreat. Dusty battled furiously with himself to sit still and wait as the Intelligence chief opened the file and began pawing its contents. At last he selected a single sheet, and leaned back with a triumphant grunt.

"Thought I was right," he said aloud. "Here's his dossier, what little we have of it."

Then he began to read from the paper.

"Ekar—name conferred upon ranking officer of Black Invader Chemical Warfare Research Department. Title, meaning highest. Real name of present holder unknown. But this man has held said position since early conquest of Asia.

"Stature, large. Features and physical characteristics usual Invader type except that left ear is missing. Reported destroyed by acid experiment. Responsible for Black Invader gas gun, sleeping gas, flame tanks and several other chemical warfare weapons. Reported (year ago) during last part of conquest of Europe to be working on development of chemical rain. (Details and further explanation missing). Speaks all languages and is reported to be a favorite of Black Invader commander-in-chief. More details to follow later."

Horner put the sheet back on the desk, stared at the ceiling.

"We never obtained any more details," he said, as though talking to himself, "That was Agent 14's report. We lost him shortly after. Ekar, eh? We certainly are up against Satan himself this time, Ayres!"

Before Dusty could make any comment the door slammed open and General Bradley came charging through. He went over to Dusty in two long strides. In his right hand he clenched a strip of paper. He shook it in front of the pilot's face.

"You fool, Ayres!" he shouted. "Don't you know that the enemy has ears as well as we have? Good God, man, because of you, your whole Group has been wiped out!"

Dusty steeled himself, and forced the words off his lips.

"Group Seven wiped out?" he echoed in a hollow voice. "When—where—how?"

The other smoothed out the paper between his fingers.

"There it is!" he roared. "Your radio to Washington Air Force H.Q. Look, read it yourself—'Group Seven abandoning present field and moving to N.H. Five!' God Almighty! Two hours ago N.H. Five was wiped out. Destroyed—like Louisville, and J Four, and Cleveland! For the love of God, why did you send that news out over the air? I tried to check back with you at the time—but couldn't make contact!"

Dusty's steel muscles relaxed, and his heart slid down from the back of his throat to its proper position. For one crazy moment he wanted to roar with laughter, and in the next he wanted to do a jig dance of sheer relief. But he did neither. Instead he grinned into General Bradley's beet-red face.

"Unless I'm very much mistaken, sir," he said, "you'll find Group Seven temporarily quartered at Albany Four."

The air force chief scowled deeper than ever. He started to speak, then cut it off and went over to the inter-office phone on Horner's desk.

"Bradley!" he barked into the built-in speaker. "Get Sampson at my office, at once!"

Fifteen seconds of silence, then he spoke again.

"Sampson? Code radio to Albany Four! Find out if Seven has—eh, what's that? Just came through? Never mind, then."

The senior air officer snapped off contact, switched his eyes to Dusty.

"You're right, Ayres," he grunted, a trifle grudgingly. "Group Seven has just reported its new position. But what the devil was your idea in sending out that crazy bit of information?"

Dusty shrugged.

"A hunch, sir, if you want to call it that," he replied. "Our area was static jammed. I figured that meant they were preparing to close in on us soon—pull the Louisville stunt. So I took a long chance, sent out that fake information—hoping that they'd listen in, and bite. Well, they did. Incidentally, Seven's field must have been passed up for N.H. Five—so it's still there when the gang wants to use it again, after this other business is cleared up."

"Possibly so," nodded the other. "You've saved your Group

from God knows what. But N.H. Five is destroyed. Read the N.H. Four infantry base report myself, not twenty minutes ago. And, it said, 'Entire N.H. Five area consumed by flames and minor explosions believed to have come from enemy aircraft.' Good God, Ayres, you save some while others are killed!"

It was all Dusty could do to keep from laughing in the senior officer's face. It was not the first time that Staff had become so "hept" up on a thing that they forgot everything else.

"I think you're mistaken, sir," he said quietly. "I know N.H. Five quite well. That's why I sent out that area position. It is between Mount Adams and Mount Madison. No troops are within fifty miles of it. And what civilian population there was in the area evacuated after the first month of war, if you'll remember."

Bradley gulped and practically rocked back on his heels. Words failed him, but not so, General Horner.

"By God, Ayres is right, Bradley!" he boomed. "Except for a branch line of the Boston and Maine, there isn't a damn thing of importance for them to destroy."

It took a minute or two for the truth to sink in, and when it did, General Bradley immediately showed his true colors. He nodded and smiled slightly.

"My apologies, Ayres," he said. "Should have known better than to go off half-cocked. Sorry. But, tell me, what about Lieutenant Brooks and Lieutenant Bolton?"

THE VERY mention of Curly's name froze Dusty's heart again. With savage determination he had been forcing his pal out of his thoughts, that he might devote all of his energies to

Curly
BROOKS

the task at hand. But now Bradley had recalled all the latent bitterness. In a few sentences he told what he knew.

"And it's all my fault, sir," he finished up sadly. "But for me, Lieutenant Brooks would still be alive. And I pray to God that he is!"

"You're wrong in one thing," Bradley corrected. "If Brooks is still alive, its due to you. It is also due to you that we still have those new designs—assuming, of course that Brooks still has his plane. Your hunch was right—there was nothing left at Cleveland. Pratt's experimental laboratory was completely demolished along with everything else. Had the planes remained, they would have gone too."

All of which brought little joy to Dusty. Damn the planes anyway! The life of Curly Brooks could not be gauged by numbers of planes. Those dirty rats—what in hell could be done to trip them up? They—

He cut off the thought with a gasp.

"If I did it once, maybe I can do it again!" he said out loud.

The other two looked at him, asked the question in the same voice.

"Do what again?"

In his excitement Dusty forgot all about titles of rank. He took a step closer to them.

"Listen, this Ekar!" he began, "he's the king-pin, and unless I'm wrong, he has a particular fancy for my scalp. And like the Hawk, he seems to have a flare for dramatics. In other words, he wants me to go out in style. And wants me to know who's doing it, hence all his trick talk to me."

"What the devil are you getting at?" frowned Horner.

"This," Dusty came right back at him. "Why did he send me that warning instead of smacking down on Group Seven? Because he wanted me to know what was coming to me. Why did he tag me from Cleveland to Louisville without doing anything? Because he wanted to get me in position, and then let me know what was going to happen to me.

"Why did he try to find out where I was headed when I was on my way here? Just to keep track of me. My fake radio message had fooled him too late, I guess. In short, he seems to be a patient cuss. He's willing to wait until the stage is set—set for him to speak his little piece on how I'm going to pass out. Well, we'll set the stage for him."

"Meaning what?" grunted Horner, his eyes skeptical.

Dusty glanced at his wrist watch before answering. The hands showed exactly twenty minutes of four.

"Give me fifteen minutes to get to the field and into the air," he said. "Then send out an S.O.S. emergency call on my wavelength instructing me to contact a bombing group over Maine-Seven, at six sharp. Repeat it three or four times so that they'll be sure to pick it up, but don't ask for a check-back. Then I won't have to give my position away."

"And what do you plan to do?" asked Bradley.

Dusty gestured.

"Play hide and seek," he said. "He's bound to show up, and the new design I'm flying will take care of everything. At any rate, if those two circle formations are with him, I'll at least be able to get a look at them. And—I'm hoping that I'll be able to tag them back to their base. Back to NF-Eight."

The two generals continued to scowl dubiously. It was Horner who voiced the thought they undoubtedly shared.

"Why not arrange for three or four of our groups to show up and shoot the lot of them down?"

Dusty shook his head.

"As General Bradley said, sir, they've got ears and eyes, too. If he came he would spot the trap with plenty of time to spare. And—"

"But he would expect bombers!" put in Bradley.

"But not pursuit and attack planes," Dusty replied. "He'll only be looking for one pursuit job—mine! And when he spots me all alone—well, then my job begins. Frankly, it's the only move we can make right now. That, if nothing else, will pull him out into the open. And that's what we want to do."

The two generals looked at each other and, so it seemed to Dusty, sighed with reluctant resignation. Then Bradley spoke.

"Very well, Ayres," he said. "After this night of hell anything is worth at least one try. For the time being, forget what I said about promoting you to Staff. Your judgment will have to be your own destiny for a while—and ours, too. But for God's sake, contact us the instant you need help—of any kind. Understand?"

Dusty was already on his way to the door.

"Yes sir," he said over his shoulder. Then looking straight at General Horner, "Jack's tough, sir. He'll come through—I feel it!"

And with those words of encouragement for the thought-tortured chief of Intelligence, he shouldered out through the door and raced for the elevators. Sixty-nine stories lower he stepped out into the lobby, darted through the entrance doors and ran down the long flight of stone steps.

As was the department ruling at all times, several fast staff cars were parked and waiting at the curb. Dusty signaled the nearest one and climbed in back. But as he slapped the limousine door shut he suddenly heard some one shouting his name. Jerking around he saw out the fear window a blurred figure running diagonally toward him from across the street.

The sedan had already leaped into motion, though Dusty had given no orders to the uniformed figure on the other side of the glass partition. He cursed, swung around and reached out a hand for the window knob.

"Hey! Wait a minute! Who the devil told you to—?"

The rest of the words would not come off his lips. And his hand reaching out to slide open the glass partition became as a bar of lead that dropped heavily at his side. His head was floating away from his shoulders, and a crazy conglomeration of stars danced in front of his eyes. Then a great roaring set up in his ears. Flames seared his throat and lungs. A heavy, parching nothingness pushed him down and down and down.

And then the earth split open and he went spinning into a great yawning abyss of flickering crimson.

CHAPTER 7
DIVING DEAD MAN

W HEN HE again opened his eyes his first impression was that someone was throwing water in his face. And the impression was correct. Some one was doing exactly that—throwing water in his face and swabbing it off with a dripping rag.

A million trip-hammers were at work on the inside of his head, and everything was a confused conglomeration of blurs and moving shadows. But somehow he managed to fling up a protesting hand and grab the dripping rag being pulled down over his face. Instantly it was removed, and not by his own efforts. And from out of the fog came a voice.

"Thank God you're coming around. Here—easy! Take some of this."

The mouth of a flask was wedged between Dusty's teeth, and liquid fire trickled down his throat. It made him cough and gag and sputter. But regardless, it did the one thing for which it was intended. It cleared his head and abated the dull aching considerably.

"There! Howzit now, skipper?"

It was then that Dusty realized that he was blinking owlishly into the grinning features of Biff Bolton. Unable to believe his eyes, he gaped at the big pilot, then let his eyes rove about.

He found himself propped up against the rear wall of a dilapidated shed. The first faint rays of a dawn sun were filtering through innumerable cracks in the walls, lighting up the interior with dull-gray illumination. Directly in front of him two hawk-featured figures in U.S. motor transport uniforms sat on the floor, tied securely back to back. And beyond them was something that jerked a gulp of utter amazement from out of his throat. It was a small semi-wing cabin biplane, painted jet black, except for the two sides of the barrel fuselage upon which was a white bulls-eye with the Black Invader flag painted in the middle.

Nine million different cockeyed thoughts pounding around in his brain, Dusty hardly realized that he staggered up onto his feet. It was only the warning voice of Biff Bolton that made him conscious of what he had done.

"Steady, skipper! Just get your breath first."

Dusty stared dully at the grinning features again, then furrowed his brows.

"You, Biff?" he managed to get out. "Wait! Give me that again."

He took the flask that the big pilot still held in his hand, put it to his lips and took a big swallow. The second swallow doubled the helpful effect of the first.

"Now I know I must be alive," he choked out, and handed the flask back. "What the hell happened, and how did you get into the picture? I—my God, man, Group Seven! What happened?"

"Nothing," grinned Bolton. "We moved to Albany without any trouble. Then—well, you hadn't ordered me to stay, and I got thinking about Jack Horner—him being hurt maybe. Anyway, I high-balled for Washington military field and started to ask questions. But no soap. A corporal guarding your ship wouldn't take the muzzle of his gun off my stomach—even when he could see I had a ship like yours.

"And he told me just as much about you as a clam would. So I left him and headed for Signal H.Q. From there I went to the naval hospital. And then, hearing that you'd left with General Horner, I headed for the War Department Building."

The big pilot paused long enough to suck in a deep breath and grin.

"Saw you getting into that car, and yelled," he said. "Guess you didn't hear me, so I made a leap for the trunk rack, and made it. Figured that maybe you were headed for the field. So I decided to go along too. Figured something was in the wind— you sure came out of that place fast. Anyway, when the car stops, we're just outside this place—damned if I know where it is. Not very far from Washington, though. Anyway—"

Bolton stopped long enough to jerk a thumb at the pair tied together on the floor.

"Anyway," he went on, "one of these lads comes running out to help the guy back of the wheel pull you out. One look at you, and—well, maybe I got mad. I knew something was screwy, so—well, them not seeing me soon enough was their tough luck. I've been worried about you, so I haven't had time to make the babies talk. Huh—you in back there, out cold, and me riding the trunk rack and not knowing it! Boy, was I a dumb lug! Could have helped you a lot sooner."

Dusty had to grin.

"You dumb, Biff?" he echoed. "Then I wish to hell I could be

82

dumb! Maybe I'd do something right, once in a blue moon. I walked into that gas trap like a ten year old. But thank God it was only gas, and not some of their deadly stuff. If—"

He stopped short and stiffened.

"Now that's an idea!" he murmured, as though to himself. "These lads didn't want me to die. Maybe they got orders."

He turned toward the pair on the floor, stopped short and shot a questioning look back at Biff.

"Curly?" he got out with a tremor. "Did you hear—?"

Bolton's sad shake of his head stopped him.

"No, skipper. Not a thing. But ground searching parties have been sent out to where I saw him going down."

DUSTY STOOD perfectly still, and clamped down hard on his jangled nerves. Then he went over to the pair on the floor. A closer look at their faces was proof positive that Biff had done a very thorough job. Had a couple of riveting hammers been substituted for the big fellow's fists the job couldn't have been any more thorough. Dusty fixed agate eyes on the one on the left. One eye glared back at him. The other was neatly closed and would remain so for some time.

Suddenly Dusty shot out a hand and smashed the palm across the man's face.

"Ekar?" he snapped. "He sent you?"

The man groaned, clenched his teeth and said nothing. Dusty sensed Biff Bolton at his side. The big pilot spoke in a grating voice.

"You're being too kind, skipper. This is the way—with your knuckles."

Bolton's fist went up and came down vertically from the man's temple to jaw bone.

"Spit it out, bum!"

Biff's command was partially drowned out by the choking cry of pain.

"Don't—don't!" screamed the man. And then he broke into gibbering phrases in Black Invader jargon.

But, he stopped them almost immediately as Biff's fist went up again.

"You'll get it baby!" roared the big pilot, "unless you talk!"

The Black agent looked beseechingly at Dusty, but there was no pity in the Yank ace's heart, and the Black must have realized it immediately. He gulped and started pouring out the words.

"I do not know Ekar. Of him I have heard, yes. But I do not know. To me come only orders. From whom I do not know. It is the way we work. The orders are to try and capture you. But I have failed. Death I do not fear. But no—no more pain. Kill me, but keep this madman from me!"

Dusty said nothing. He nudged Biff as the big fellow's fist went up again and walked around to the other Black. The sight was the same. Features hammered to a purple, bleeding pulp, and one good eye glazed with terror.

"You!" Dusty shot at him. "Let's hear your little piece!"

The man shook his head vigorously, outwardly wincing from the pain that movement caused.

"Less than he I know!" he babbled out wildly. "For me it is only to fly. He says, and I fly. Meanwhile, I stay here."

Eyeing him a second Dusty went back to the first one.

"You're doing very nicely!" he said in a hard voice. "Now go right on talking—where were you going to take me, eh?"

The Black, eyes on Biff's ever-ready fist, cringed and opened his mouth.

"Do not know—do not know!" he streamed desperately. "The orders are but to fly you north—at fifty thousand feet. That is all—just north from here at fifty thousand feet."

"Goofer dust!" growled Biff. "You lie, you damn ape, and you know it! Come on—spit it all out!"

The fist was on its way down as the man screamed.

"No, no! It is the truth—it is the truth! We are to fly straight north. Perhaps they will tell us later what next to do."

"Tell you how?" Dusty rapped at him.

"Radio," came the quavering answer. "Perhaps find us in the air. It is only for us to obey orders!"

Biff brought his fist down, just for luck, and the man howled with pain. Dusty hardly heard it. Straightening up slowly he stared hard at the cabin plane, countless thoughts chasing each other around in his brain.

"It's a stall, skipper! That rat's lying, sure as hell!"

Biff's voice interrupted Dusty's dancing thoughts. He glanced at his pal and shook his head.

"Nope, Biff," he said. "I think the bum is telling the truth. They work that way—left hand not knowing what the right's doing."

"But hell!" exploded Bolton. "It's goofy! Just fly due north with you aboard? When're they going to come down? At the North Pole meteorological station?"

85

Dusty glanced at his watch and grunted. It was eighteen minutes of six. Eighteen minutes more and he was supposed to make the fake bombing group contact over Main-Seven.

Somehow as he mulled his original plan over in his brain, it seemed very flat and pointless. If this Ekar tramp had given orders for him to be kidnaped, and if the bum knew he had landed at Washington military field, he would realize that there was a catch in the fake radio order the instant he heard it.

Dusty's memory suddenly raced backwards. Hell, was he ever going to use his head? Of course Ekar had kept tabs on his whereabouts. He'd done that with his station directional finder as he faked a Two-Four-Two call from Curly.

"The hell with it!" snorted Dusty aloud. "Damned if I won't play it his way, then!"

He looked at Biff.

"Pile these tramps in the car outside and take them to Horner," he ordered. "Maybe through them he can get the skunk who knifed Jack. Yeah, Jack was knifed while contacting me. General Horner will tell you the rest of the story. I haven't got time just now, kid."

The big pilot didn't move.

"What are you planning, skipper?" he grunted out.

Dusty nodded toward the Blacks.

"Going to pinch hit for them," he said. "Kidnap myself and fly myself north. I've a hunch things will start happening then."

Bolton ran his tongue over his lower lip.

"Four years in the service, and I've never disobeyed an order yet," he said. "But, these mugs stay here skipper. I'm going with you!"

Dusty started to shake his head but checked the movement. After all, if it hadn't been for Biff—

"Okay, Biff," he nodded. "Perhaps you're right. Just make sure that these lads will stay here. And I'll get these shed doors open."

Less than three minutes later, Dusty was climbing in through the small cabin door. Bolton was right behind him, tentatively rubbing the knuckles of his right fist with the palm of his left hand. Dusty glanced toward the rear of the shed. The two Blacks were on their sides, bound tightly from neck to ankles. Their eyes were closed and their mouths sagged open, Both were listening to the birdies.

"Sorry, skipper," came Bolton's grunt. "But I just naturally couldn't stop myself. And it may be awhile before we get back."

DUSTY MADE no comment. Sliding into the seat, he punched the starter with his toe, caught the engine on the first rev, and released the wheel brakes. With inches to spare at the wing-tips the plane rolled out onto a small square of dawn-lighted field.

A minute to give the engine a "break" and Dusty rammed the throttle forward. Seconds later he was clearing the treetops at the far end and streaking up through a thin ground mist. Before it became too thick he turned in the seat and glanced downward. To his left was the Potomac winding its way into the nation's capital. To his right rear were the outskirts of Georgetown. And directly ahead, Rockville.

IT MUST BE CURLY!

His exact position ascertained, he swung due north and went plowing up through the mist. It thickened into heavy fog at ten thousand, thinned a bit at twenty, thickened some more at thirty, and finally became clear sun-tinted air at thirty seven thousand.

But Dusty did not level off until the altimeter needle showed on the Black Invader-manufactured dial the American equivalent of fifty thousand feet. When it did, he turned and spoke to Bolton for the first time since the take-off.

"Listen, Biff," he said. "Here's a rough outline of all I know."

Then in as few words as possible he told the story of Jack Horner, and of Ekar's dossier.

"I'm betting that we're due to meet this Ekar bum in the air before long," he finished up. "But I may be wrong. Damned if it isn't becoming a habit with me. However, if we don't, we're going straight through to NF-Eight. One thing is in our favor at least—that's this ship. And when—"

He left the rest hanging. The red signal light on the radio panel was blinking.

"Company so soon?" he grunted, and flipped out his free hand.

The instant he snapped on contact, and spun the wave-length dial, the cabin speaker unit crackled out words.

"Calling Two-Four-Two! Calling Two-Four-Two!"

Over and over again the message was repeated. Dusty toned down volume, grinned at Bolton, and looked at the directional finder dial needle. It showed that the station broadcasting was located between seven and eight hundred miles north-northeast of his position. In short, close to Maine-Seven area. Dusty chuckled harshly.

"Damned if he didn't fall for that fake bombing group contact after all!" he yelled to Bolton. "And now he's trying to pick me up on Curly's and my signal. Hell, if I only knew that Curly was okay!"

Bolton made no comment. He sat staring hard at the cabin speaker unit, brows furrowed and head cocked on one side.

"Tune her up a bit, skipper," he said suddenly. "Something queer about that sound. Not clear at all. Sounds muffled—like it was close to a static-jammed area."

The big pilot was right. As Dusty turned on volume and the repeated call came through louder, he too noticed the same thing. It was as though the broadcaster was yelling through cotton into a rain barrel. Even the harsh, rasping voice tone of Ekar, the unknown, was missing.

And then suddenly, it died out and the radio went silent. Dusty made no attempt to pick it up on any other wave-length. His plans had met with another right-about-face, but that didn't matter a bit. Tapping rudder and stick he veered around until the nose was headed dead-on for the Maine-Eight area. Then he stuck the nose down slightly to add speed to the craft and crouched grimly over the stick.

Just what he'd do when he met the mysterious Ekar he had no idea at that moment. Perhaps he'd shoot him down—perhaps he'd play the waiting game and let the Black chemical warfare expert make the first move—perhaps he'd do any one of a number of things. He didn't know. What he did know, was that somewhere far ahead there in the blue, action was awaiting him. It would be action face to face this time—no confounded put-putting around in a sea of dark night. No sir, not by a damn sight!

"Eyes peeled, Biff!" he yelled back over his shoulder. "Shout the instant you spot anything. We're not in a pursuit job you know."

"Right!" came back the short answer.

AND THEN began a long period of tensed and silent waiting. A thousand times Dusty spotted swarms of Black Darts, only to realize a split second later that they were simply cloud scud being burned into oblivion by the sun. And an equal number of times he cursed the slowness of all cabin planes and the one he was flying in particular. Even with the additional speed made possible by the shallow dive he held the plane in, the craft seemed to virtually float through the air like a free balloon at the mercy of prevailing winds.

One hour, maybe one year, and then Biff Bolton's heavy hand slammed down on his shoulder, and the big fellow's voice cried out hoarsely.

"*There*—to the right—just coming around that cloud bank!"

Dusty snapped his aching eyes around to the direction mentioned. For the first few seconds the sun blinded him. But as he "covered" it, one eye closed and thumb to the other, he saw a small blur plunging swiftly toward him. Sight and action became one. There was no time to study the approaching plane. Thumping down hard on right rudder and banging the stick over, he flung the cabin plane into a spinning half roll, then came out heading directly toward the other ship. A hard grin tugging back the corners of his mouth, he slid his thumbs up to the electric trigger trips.

"Now, sweetheart!" he grated. "We'll let you make the first move."

As though the pilot of the on-coming ship, still little more than a blur in the sun's rays, had actually heard his words, twin streams of jetting flame leaped out from its pointed snout. But a second later the firing stopped and the plane nosed up for more altitude.

And it was then that truth smote Dusty's brain like a ton of brick. He was able to see the plane clearly as it went zooming up. Hardly conscious of his voice he bellowed out the words.

"That's not a Black! It's one of Pratt's designs. It's Curly—it must be Curly!"

CHAPTER 8
ACES DOWN

HARDLY HAD the words left his lips than they were echoed by Bolton's roaring voice.

"By God, you're right, you're right! Hell—look out! He means to half roll down on us!"

The last, as far as Dusty was concerned, was unnecessary. He had already seen the thin, tapered wing monoplane start to whip over and down. With every ounce of his strength he pulled the nose up. And at the same instant he snapped on radio contact and grabbed the transmitter tube.

"Hold it, kid, hold it!" he roared.

The sleek monoplane streaking downward veered sharply off to the side and came cutting around as though its pilot intended to take up wing-tip formation. Across the air space Dusty could just faintly make out Curly Brooks' face behind the orange peel glass cockpit cowl. And a split second later he heard his pal's voice cackle out of the cabin speaker unit.

"What the hell? I've been hunting you for hours!"

Dusty started to reply, but suddenly he became conscious of a "fuzzy" note in Curly's transmission. It was like a hour or so ago when he'd heard the repeated Two-Four-Two call. Now he knew that it meant but one thing. A powerful station, somewhere, was listening in on the same wave-length. Realization caused the blood to dance through his veins.

"Story later!" he snapped into the transmitter tube. "Right now, scram!"

The monoplane "mushed" in closer and Curly's face became quite clear to Dusty. The lean pilot was scowling darkly. Then he spoke again.

"Scram yourself! Plenty trouble north! Two formations of radio-controlled ships over Maine-Seven. Supported by enemy pursuit group. Got a couple, and lit out!"

Dusty hated himself for his next words. But, he had to say them. There was no way out of it.

"Shut up! Scram! Orders!"

For perhaps five seconds the monoplane flew wingtip to wingtip with Dusty's plane. Then it suddenly swung up in a loop, rolled off the top and went streaking away to the south. And as it did, the cabin speaker unit cracked out words.

"Yes sir. I'll throttle to your speed, and lead you south!"

Heart pounding with pride of friendship, Dusty veered the cabin job back on its due north course, and swung off Curly's wave-length reading. Behind him, Biff Bolton grunted. And a moment later the big pilot laid a hand on his shoulder.

"Guess I'm dumb, skipper," he grunted. "What's he mean, lead you south?"

Dusty spoke without turning his head.

"He doesn't know, but he's guessing plenty. He's guessing that we're planning to slip past the Black formations up ahead. He knows that some station listened in on us. So he's making it seem that I've turned around and am heading south. In other words, passing up the Maine-Seven meeting. Dammit, wish I could have found out what happened to him."

"Yeah, me too!" echoed Bolton. "So, what next?"

"NF-Eight!" Dusty grunted. "You heard Curly—two formations radio controlled? Well, I'm adding two and two and figuring that they're controlled from NF-Eight. That's where we're heading—straight for NF-Eight. Ekar and his bums can hang around Maine-Seven until they get blue in the face for all I care."

"Maybe you're right," murmured Biff. "O.K. by me, anyway."

But Dusty wasn't listening. Hunched over the stick he stared out at the world of sun-tinted air and tried to map out a definite plan of operation. In his mind he pictured the entire NF area—its towns, hill country, small rivers, glacier-like formations, wooded sections and vast stretches of utter wilderness.

To slide down in close to NF-Eight would be simple—provided. And it was that word that creased his brows in a frown. Provided they were not picked up by Black patrols, it would be fairly simple. Under the cover of darkness it would be simple, Black patrols or no Black patrols. But in broad daylight? Hell, a pity he had wasted so much time getting started.

He glanced at his wrist watch and cursed softly. Nine hours since he'd left Group Seven's field for Cleveland Experimental, and where was he?—still taking pot shots on hunches. Yeah, he'd be hot stuff on Staff, alright! Just about dumb enough for that kind of a job!

One hour later, still in the same frame of mind, he tapped stick and rudder and veered the ship around onto a northeast by east course. He was flying at sixty two thousand and directly over (if his calculations were correct) the western tip of Anticosti Island in the Gulf of St. Lawrence. Another half hour's flying and it would be time to ease earthward.

During every minute of the flight he had kept constant vigilance of the surrounding sky. And he knew that Biff Bolton had been doing the very same thing. Yet not once had he even so much as spotted anything that might be taken for an enemy patrol—not even a single plane. True, he was flying considerably higher than the altitude of usual defense air patrols. But not seeing anything worried him. And it worried Bolton, too, as his very next words proved.

"Not so good, skipper! Seems to me we're making it too easy. Haven't seen a sign of a ship."

"Maybe luck's with us," replied Dusty with a conviction he didn't feel. "Maybe—"

At that moment the radio signal light blinked, and the cabin speaker unit gave forth sound. The sound was not in the form of words, however, it was the dot-dashing of the Black Invader secret highspeed code. It stopped abruptly, then started up again, but in a different transmitting tone. Again it stopped, and again it was taken up by a third broadcasting station.

THE INSTANT it began Dusty's eyes had snapped to the station directional finder dial. And as the third station cut off the air, his heart became as a lump of lead in his chest.

Translation of the secret signals was unnecessary. Their broadcasting positions was sufficient. The station directional finder dial told him that. One was to the north, one to the west, and one to the south. And he was flying due east toward NF-Eight. In other words, his position was known—it must be known—and a semi-circle of patrolling aircraft was closing in on him from three sides!

For a moment he was filled with a savage desire to tear earthward in the hope of being able to skid around south and slip through the cordon of enemy aircraft "tailing" him. But he squelched the idea even as it came to him. If planes were tailing him they were bound to be at varying altitudes right down to the ground. Of course, he might scrap and be lucky—break through and get back to Yank ground. But hell—NF-Eight would still be NF-Eight!

With his free fist he smashed the throttle wide open and stuck the nose down.

"Let 'em come and be damned to them!" he thundered. "I'm going through, regardless. Biff! Hang on!"

Engine roaring out a mighty song of power, wings screaming in the terrific rush of air, the plane tore down through blue space like a meteor gone absolutely crazy. Like a knife it cut through cloud layer after cloud layer, until it plunged down into the clear some twelve thousand feet above the rolling swells of the Gulf of St. Lawrence. Ahead and low down on the horizon was a dark line marking the western coast of Newfoundland.

Cutting power a bit, Dusty eased back the stick and poked the ship up into the first cloud layer. Once hidden he leveled off and set the robot for a due east course. Relaxing slightly against the back of his seat, he kept his eyes glued to the robot compass control, and his ears tuned for any sound from the cabin speaker unit.

Ten minutes dragged by and then the speaker unit spilled out high speed dot-dashing. Dusty smiled grimly and took his eyes off the compass long enough to look at Biff Bolton's strained features.

"My guess is that they've lost us," he grunted. "That dive caught them napping, and they're contacting ground stations. Hear those heavy signals? That's a powerful ground station."

"Yeah, guess it is," grunted Bolton. "But what do you plan to do? We can't hang up here all day!"

"An old trick is always good for another try," Dusty encouraged him. "They expect us from the west, so well just pay our

97

visit from the east. After all, maybe they don't know what kind of a ship they're looking for."

Bolton made no comment. He simply sat rigid, uneasy eyes fixed on the cloud mist swirling past the cabin windows.

Then, suddenly he let out a wild cry of alarm.

"Look out—look out!"

Dusty saw it too, but he was powerless to act, everything happened so fast. A dark shadow came charging toward them in the cloud mist. Like a phantom it came, then veered slightly and raced past them and was gone. The cabin ship rocked violently, threatened to go over on wing. Heart virtually still, Dusty righted the ship and pulled it back on an even keel. Then with a whistling sigh he expelled the clamped air from his lungs.

"That was too damned close!" he breathed. "Almost hit us. Some of them in the clouds, too, eh?"

As he murmured the last, he swung off robot control, took the stick himself and veered around to a course due north. The realization that Black ships were undoubtedly groping about in the cloud layer for him set his nerves to quivering. A mid-air crash would undoubtedly mean the end of everything. True, it would be tough luck for the other fellow, too. But—Dusty cut off the rest as a thought suddenly crashed home. He swung about in his seat, looked toward the rear of the cabin, then turned forward again. Reaching out his free hand, he eased back the throttle and let the ship slide into a shallow glide.

"Biff!" he snapped without turning. "There's two chutes back there. Put one on and hand me the other. Maybe we can fool these babies yet."

The cloud layer was thinning rapidly as Dusty felt Biff behind him with a vest chute pack. Holding the stick with his left hand he shoved his right hand through the vest arm hole. Then he reversed the procedure and finally clamped the vest hooks in place. By then the lower part of the ship was clear of the bottom of the cloud layer and Dusty could just faintly see below. It took him but a matter of seconds to determine his exact position.

He was about thirty miles inland from Bonavista and perhaps twice that number of miles northwest of Shoal Harbor. By straining his eyes he could see Black Invader ships standing off the coast, and below him, troop and supply encampments. But to those he only gave a quick glance. Ahead and to the left was a wide area of desolate ground.

Easing back the stick he nosed up into the clouds again.

"Here's the plan, Biff," he said speaking rapidly. "Getting down in the ship is too much of a risk. We'd probably be spotted. Now five minutes flying from here is barren ground—hills covered with rocks and scrub trees. When we get over it, I'm going to swing the ship back toward Shoal Harbor, and strap the stick so that it will climb. Then we go overboard. Make a free fall as long as you can. Then, well… open the chutes."

"Got you!" came Biff's steady voice. "Think they wouldn't be able to spot the free fall, eh?"

Dusty nodded.

"That's what I'm hoping, anyway. Now, get over by the door and get set."

As Biff turned away Dusty started easing down through the clouds again. His nerves tingled throughout his entire body, and memory raced back to the time when he and Jack Horner had bailed out in the dead of night over the Devil's Factory area. He clamped down on his nerves and forced his lips back in a grin.

"This'll be even easier!" he said to himself.

And then he dismissed everything but thoughts of immediate action from his mind. The cabin plane had slid below the cloud layer again. Directly below lay a wide area of God-forsaken countryside.

"Ready, Biff!" Dusty grunted, and slamming on throttle he sent the plane curving around and up into the clouds for the third time.

The instant the swirling mist engulfed the ship he slid out of the seat and hooked the triple safety belt straps over the stick. Then one hand gripping the rip-ring of his vest chute pack he went over to where Biff Bolton waited at the cabin door. He grinned encouragement at his friend.

"Let's go, buzzard!" he said. "Hang onto my right with your left. Better stick together as long as we can. Oke—out and down to terra firma!"

Biff returned the grin, swung down the ratchet gear handle that opened the door against the slipstream, and catching hold of Dusty's hand, stepped out into thin air.

HANDS LOCKED in a death-like grip, the two of them went spinning head over heels downward. Icy air slashed and ripped at them as they hurtled downward. Clenching his teeth against the cold, Dusty strained his wind-fluttered eyes at the ground. He was falling head-first, his feet and legs perpendicular above him. In a dull, abstract way he was conscious of the sharp pain in the back of his neck caused by twisting his head back so that he could see the ground.

Wind whistled and roared in his ears. Then, as for no reason at all, his body twisted over so that he was falling broadside to the ground. Everything became deathly quiet, but only for a second or two. A trick of the wind currents shot his feet up to the vertical again, and he continued to plunge head-first downward.

Like a giant carpet of spotted gray, brown and black, the ground came sweeping up. One thousand, two thousand, or three thousand? He couldn't tell. The rush of wind past him watered his eyes and made everything a swimming blur. He clamped down hard with his teeth; forced himself to count ten. Then he jerked his hand free from Bolton's grasp.

"Pull, Biff, pull!"

He didn't even hear his own words. He only knew that he had said them. But as they had boomed off his lips, he had instinctively yanked down hard on his rip-ring clutched tightly in his left hand. A second and then a faint swishing sound. Then an unseen giant hand reached down grabbed him about the waist and jerked him back toward the clouds. A moment later he was fighting for breath and slowly swinging back and forth like a human pendulum suspended from a taut umbrella of shimmering silk.

Breath back to normal, eyes cleared of watering, he twisted about in the vest harness and searched the surrounding air. For a moment his heart stood still. Biff Bolton was nowhere to be

A TANGLED MASS CAME RUSHING OUT OF THE CLOUD LAYER

seen. God, had Biff continued his free fall—continued it straight into the ground? He himself was only fifteen hundred feet or so above it.

And then with a grunt of relief he saw the big pilot. Bolton was about seventy-five yards in back of him and a couple of hundred feet up. He was waving his arms in happy salute. Dusty waved back then switched his gaze toward the general direction of Shoal Harbor.

He was too low to see anything clearly. In fact it was practically time to flex his knees and get set for a landing on a barren

103

hill slope directly below. But he risked a more searching glance toward the NF-Eight area.

It was in that instant it happened.

The cloud layer suddenly spewed out belching flame and smoke, and a roar of sound smashed against his ear-drums. Split seconds later a tangled mass came rushing out of the cloud layer far over toward Shoal Harbor.

It seemed to part in two, one-half slithering down this way, the other half slithering down another. But though the distance was great, Dusty's eyes saw and a shout of triumph burst from his throat. One-half of the flaming, smoking mass was the crumpled ruins of the semi-wing cabin biplane. The other half was the crumpled rains of a Black Dart pursuit.

As though by magic, an instant later, a dozen or more Black planes came tearing down out of the cloud layer, and in ring-around-the-rosy fashion they started circling about the flaming cabin plane.

The maneuvers brought a harsh laugh from Dusty's lips.

"Yoo-hoo!" he mimicked. "Nobody knows where we are!"

The last he ended in a yelp, as he glanced downward. The jagged tip of a lightning-split tree trunk was right smack under him. In a flash he shot up both hands, and "spilled" air from the chute silk on the off side. The effort swung his body clear of the jagged point. But it raced up past him with bare inches to spare and sliced through the chute itself.

There was a rip of silk, and Dusty dropped like a stone for a good ten feet. He had only time to half flex his legs when he hit the ground. It was sloping and he went skidding off like a bobsled taking a bank too high. Frantically he flung out both hands and grabbed at scrub bushes, but the thin branches slid through his clutching fingers as though they were greased.

Down the hill slope he shot like a toboggan on a sheet-ice slide. And then suddenly an unseen giant grabbed his legs, another grabbed his chest, and both jerked in opposite directions. Instantly, downward movement stopped. And with heart slamming furiously and lungs aching for air, he lay staring glassy-eyed up the slope at shredded silk and fray shroud lines snubbed tightly about a rotted tree trunk.

CHAPTER 9
THE ONE-EARED KILLER

PERHAPS IT was two minutes, perhaps five, that he lay there inert, desperately trying to collect his thoughts. Presently the shredded silk and shroud lines took on a definite meaning to him. With an effort he pulled himself up to a sitting position, fumbled with the vest clamp hooks, and managed to wiggle out of the harness. Then he slowly got to his feet and took stock of himself.

One entire sleeve of his tunic was missing, to say nothing of miscellaneous buttons and so forth. His right field boot had been slit from top to ankle. There was a goose egg just over his left temple, and both hands and wrists were scratched and bleeding in a dozen different places. There was no mirror to confirm it, but his face felt like the battle ground of a couple of alley cats. But there were no bones broken, and his service automatic (whatever help it might be at the moment) was still in its holster.

Pulling out a handkerchief he wiped his face and hands as best he could.

"Still a bright lad, aren't you?" he snarled at himself. "Have to go sightseeing, instead of looking where you're going. Hell, hope Biff used his head, anyway."

Climbing back up to the lightning-split tree trunk, he mentally pictured his last few moments in the air. Biff had been in back of him then. That meant that he'd come down on the far side of the slope.

Starting up toward the crest, he had traveled but twenty yards when suddenly the roar of an airplane engine blasted against his ear-drums. He couldn't see the plane. It was still out of sight beyond the crest of the hill. But he didn't lose a second in hurling himself flat and rolling under the protecting branches of a large clump of scrub growth.

Hardly had he stopped rolling when a plane tore past overhead. It was a mid-wing monoplane with a short stubby fuselage, and painted jet black. He saw it and lost it again in the matter of a split second. But for safety's sake he stayed right where he was until the throbbing of the engine faded out in the distance.

"Break number two for the poor people!" he grunted, scrambling out and starting up the slope again. "At least he didn't spot either of us or he would have hung around."

When he reached the crest he stopped and peered hard down the opposite slope. It was more densely covered with growth than the side upon which he had come down. At the bottom the heavy growth changed into brown reed grass. Beyond that was a twenty-foot-wide shallow stream. But there was not a single sight of moving life.

For a moment Dusty gazed at the scene in frowning perplexity as he toyed with the possibility of being wrong in his calculations as to where Biff Bolton had landed. And then, as a branch cracked off to his left, he whirled, right hand darting for his gun. He relaxed instantly as Biff Bolton crawled out from behind some fallen tree trunks.

"See that bum who passed over, skipper?" was the big pilot's first remark.

Dusty nodded, and gave his pal a quick eye inspection. Bolton had obviously used his head. He looked a bit wind-blown, and there were a couple of gobs of mud here and there on his uniform, but apart from that he was in A-1 condition. Then Bolton spoke again, as though suddenly conscious of Dusty's appearance.

"Gosh, skipper! You hurt?"

Dusty shook his head savagely.

"No," he said. "It's not my fault though. By the way, did you duck undercover in time?"

"That Black ship, you mean? I hope to tell you I did! But what do we do now?"

Dusty stared moodily off toward the NF-Eight area, over thirty miles away. He couldn't see it, of course, because of the hilly shrub-covered country in between, but he could picture in his mind what it was like.

"We can do one of two things, Biff," he said. "Start traveling in daylight, and risk being caught. Or hole up here until light fall and make it under the cover of darkness."

Then he added by way of encouragement:

"At least we got here, and we're still alive."

Bolton toed absently at a clump of dirt.

"If you mean I need a rest," he grunted, "forget it, skipper! Besides, being as how we don't know just what we're looking for, seems to me that daylight is a good time to look. If they fell for that stunt of yours—jumping and sending the ship back, hoping one of 'em would smack into it—we haven't got so much to worry us as we had before."

"That's true!" nodded Dusty slowly. Then in a dubious voice. "I wonder if they did fall for that—if they did figure we were in it. Hell, the whole thing has so many cockeyed ifs, ands, and buts, that it's driving me screwy. Damned if I don't feel as though we've been playing into their hands right from the start!"

"And you are correct! Don't move—either of you!"

Even as the harsh voice rang out behind him, Dusty saw Bolton stiffen and his hand streak for his gun, stop, and drop limply to his side.

"Much better!" cracked the unseen owner of the voice. "Hands above your heads, please! Quick!"

Dusty raised his hands, saw the grim reckless look that flooded Biff Bolton's face.

"Biff! Up with those hands, sap!"

Then Dusty turned.

TWENTY YARDS away stood five men in the uniform of

Black Invaders. Four of them wore the insignia of rank-and-file infantrymen. But the fifth wore officer's insignia and Black air force wings on his left chest. He was a good two inches taller than any of the others, who were about Dusty's height, and he was built in proportion. All that was included in Dusty's first impression, before he noticed the face.

When he did notice it a ripple of tensed excitement shot through him. The face was slightly hawk-featured, yet not altogether unpleasant to look at. The eyes were set wide from the nose and held a copperish glint in their unfathomable depths. The lips were not of the usual Black Invader thickness. And right now they were drawn back in a pleasant smile, revealing a perfect set of unusually white teeth. The right ear stuck out a trifle—and the left ear was missing!

Ekar, the mysterious and self-styled avenger of the Black Hawk!

As that truth struck home to Dusty, the man began to speak.

"So at last we meet, Captain Ayres! I must say, though, that your appearance does not exactly fit your reputation. Just a trifle unkempt, yes?"

Dusty made no reply. Two of the soldiers had advanced and were relieving Biff and him of their guns. Meanwhile the action was covered by the ugly snub-nosed gas-gun in Ekar's right hand. Then, as the soldiers stepped back, he nodded.

"You may lower your hands, now. You've undergone quite enough physical exertion for awhile. In fact, you may even sit down, if you like. I intend to become well-acquainted before we move on."

Dusty made no move to sit down. Hands jammed in pockets, he stared speculatively at this strange personage. The man was the distinct opposite of everything he had pictured him to be. Except for a similarity in tone of voice, he was a direct contrast to the Black Hawk. No savage gloating, no berserk rage blazing in his eyes, and no sneers and snarls and crazy twisting of his lips. In fact, the man might almost be an American—only he wasn't!

"Do sit down, Captain Ayres. I really do not intend to kill you immediately."

The Yank pilot shrugged, and squatted down on the ground. Biff Bolton followed suit, and Ekar broadened his smile and nodded genial approval.

"Perhaps that last surprises you, captain?" he asked. "Particularly after our meeting last night? Well, to be perfectly honest, if certain things had not happened I probably would shoot you right now."

Dusty forced a hard grin to his lips.

"Thanks for the postponement," he said dryly. "And what happened that makes you so kind-hearted?"

The other gestured airily with his free hand.

"Trivial things," he said. "But nevertheless of certain major importance. You will realize their significance at a later time. Right now I simply want to impress upon you how utterly pointless and childish your actions have been. I wonder when you Americans will realize that war is not a schoolboy's game, but requires constant and perpetual consideration of every single detail and item involved."

Dusty shrugged and answered in the same jocular tone.

"Oh, probably when we get tired of having you bums hanging around our front doorstep."

Had it been the Hawk, his eyes would undoubtedly have blazed up, and he might have slashed out with his gun. But not so, Ekar, the avenger. He laughed heartily and shook his head.

"But, captain!" he cried, "we bums, as you call us, insist upon coming inside the house, you see! And that is exactly what we are going to do—enter the house, without destroying it any more than we are forced to."

A hidden meaning behind the words sent a tremor zipping through Dusty. He put the question in an easy conversational tone, but his eyes were riveted on the other's face.

"And just how do you think you could destroy that house?"

"Ah!" the Black purred softly. "I see, you understand the inference. How, you ask? Think back only to last night, captain. We could very easily do the same to every square inch of your country. My newest chemical compound is the most destructive element in the world! But—what is the sense of reducing a country you intend to occupy and govern to dust and smouldering ashes? None whatsoever. Only fools would consider it."

"Yeah," nodded Dusty. "And maybe the people who live in that country might do something about stopping you."

""Yes, they might," nodded Ekar in pleasant agreement. "But, our mutual train of thought is wandering. Take yourself as an example, captain. I have sworn to kill you—and I shall! But killing you is a personal matter. It must in no way jeopardize the fulfillment of our basic plans of conquest. You follow me?"

"Nope," answered Dusty shortly. "Why not draw me a picture?"

"I will," was the prompt reply. "A word picture. Killing you and wiping out your field, and comrades, would have been all right. But you went to Cleveland. Killing you there, or later in the air, would have been all right too. Credit to you—you escaped me. I trailed you to Washington. And there my personal desires were stopped dead still. Killing you is one thing, but the destruction of your very beautiful and important seat of government, is something entirely different. Oh yes, I could very easily have reduced Washington to ruins—I can do it any time I wish—but, I am only one of many, and our cause is not governed by my wishes alone."

THE MAN paused for breath and Dusty fought in the involuntary shudder hat rippled through him. The devil was right! If what happened at Louisville Base, J Four Factory, and Cleveland Experimental was anything to base truth upon, he could have wiped Washington, D.C. clean off the map. The Yank pilot forced another grin to his lips.

"Again thanks," he grunted. "So what? Why didn't you let me know it was personal? I wouldn't have waited so long."

But Ekar wasn't looking at him. The Black's narrowed eyes were fixed on Biff Bolton. His words, however, were directed at Dusty.

"Your companion is nervous, captain. Also of small importance to me. If his fingers get so much as an inch nearer that stone, I shall kill him instantly!"

In spite of himself, Dusty jerked his head toward Biff. The

big pilot, face beet-red with thwarted rage, was slowly pulling his big paw away from a stone the size of a baseball. Dusty didn't say anything. He simply gave Biff one good look. The big fellow swallowed and grunted.

"Oke! Skip it!"

When Dusty turned back to Ekar, the Black was again smiling pleasantly.

"In answer to your last question, captain," he said. "I really did not have the opportunity. And by then our agents had begun to carry out their orders. Incidentally, I don't know the details as yet—how you did it, I mean. But did you think that we had only two agents in Washington? Five minutes after you took off in that plane—our plane—I knew it. And when I received the agent's report, I knew exactly where you were heading. I would have thought that you'd realized that your habit of invading Black territory in a Black plane would sometime come to an end!"

Dusty made no comment. Though he maintained an outward calm, he was inwardly raging at himself. He felt like a kid who has been caught with his hand in the jam jar. Ekar was playing him for a perfect sap. And the hell of it was, he had acted the part to perfection.

He forced out a scornful laugh.

"If you knew all about my movements," he said, "then why did you waste fuel hanging around Maine-Seven? I heard that you were there, you know."

"I was not there, captain," the Black replied placidly. "Since shortly after midnight I have been here, awaiting your arrival.

113

You see, from a careful study of your past ventures, I knew that you would come here. Either as a guest of our agents, or by yourself. But for caution's sake I had some of my pilots gather at Maine-Seven. What is the American expression? Oh yes, playing both ends toward the middle."

Dusty was on the point of ribbing him with Curly's victories at Maine-Seven, but checked himself in time. Instead, he smiled.

"Damn clever of you to figure that I'd come down right at this spot!" he snapped.

"On the contrary, captain, it was simply a matter of logical deduction. Circumstances forced us to try and capture you alive. Otherwise we would have killed you, sent you flaming earthward, long before you reached this island. I frankly admit that you eluded those following you once you reached the island. But that was to be expected. However, knowing full well that you would not be fool enough to land in any populated area, we simply set a watch for you in the unpopulated areas. I myself saw you jump, captain. So did one of my pilots in the air. But even then it might have been difficult for us to have found you in this wilderness had you not assisted us."

The man paused. Dusty stared at him.

"And just how did we assist you?"

The Black pointed first to one side of the slope, and then to the other.

"Your parachutes," he said quietly. "My pilot saw them on the ground, radioed me, and then flew directly over this spot. Being familiar with this area, I was able to arrive posthaste. And here I am!"

EKAR'S CASUALLY spoken words echoed and re-echoed mockingly inside Dusty's brain. He glanced at Biff, and saw the look of baffled defeat stamped on the big fellow's face. Perhaps it was sight of Bolton's bitter misery that served to strengthen his own slipping courage. At any rate, he got to his feet, squared his shoulders and looked the Black straight in the eye.

"Okay!" he snapped. "You've had your party. Shoot and be damned to you! But this officer with me is a legitimate prisoner. I forced him to come along with me."

Biff let out the roar of a bull, and leaped to his feet.

"The hell you did, skipper! By God, I'll take what you take!"

The Black seemed delighted with their actions.

"Such *esprit de corps* is most commendable," he said. "And it is really a shame that it must be wasted. I promise you both death—but not right now. I repeat, circumstances forced us to capture you alive. Those same circumstances force us to keep you alive, for the time being."

Though the death sentence had been passed on him, even a temporary postponement was a ray of hope to Dusty. Memory flashed back to Major Drake's words—"A lot can happen in a very short space of time." And after all, General Horner and General Bradley knew he was heading for NF-Eight. The longer he and Biff occupied Ekar's time, the more time for Horner and Bradley to do something. Also, there was another tiny thread of hope—Curly. But hell, what could Curly possibly do? Learn the true story, come a-flying—and get caught, or killed.

With a savage inward effort Dusty brushed that thought from his mind.

"You win," he grinned at the Black. "I'm curious. Why delay the shooting party?"

"For a very important reason, Captain Ayres," replied Ekar. "And now, I must ask you to submit while my men prepare you for a short cross-country journey."

The Black, not taking his eyes off the two Yanks, spat some of his native jargon out the corner of his mouth. Instantly two of the soldiers stepped forward, and pulled out lengths of wired cord from their tunic pockets. A minute or so later, both Biff and Curly had their wrists bound chain-gang style behind their backs, and each of the soldiers gripped the slack end of the cord. Coming forward, Ekar calmly inspected the job, and nodded his approval. Then he walked around in front of Dusty.

"They will lead the way, captain," he said, pointing at the two soldiers who still stood in their original positions. "You and your comrade will follow them. Please banish all thought of escape. There will be three of us behind you. Two, holding the reins that bind you, you might say, and myself, holding this ever-ready gas-gun. You understand?"

Dusty was conscious of a new light that had seeped into the Black's eyes. It was cold, flinty, merciless—a look that was reflecting the true nature of the inner man for the first time.

The Yank returned the look, steadily, and nodded.

"We understand," he said tight-lipped. "But I'm still curious—why the parade?"

The Black shrugged.

"Orders, captain," he said, a half smile on his lips. "There is one who desires personal talk with you—about a most important matter. You have met him before. He is known as Fire-Eyes, Emperor of the World! Now march!"

CHAPTER 10
FIRE-EYES

FIRE-EYES! THE name rang in Dusty's ears like a four-alarm fire-gong as he and Biff started forward in the wake of the two Black soldiers. Grimly he tried to collect his exploded thoughts and get a hold on himself. Two minutes ago the spark of hope had flared up brightly. Death had been temporarily postponed. But the reason?—Fire-Eyes! The very thought of that world destroyer slammed his spirits down to rock bottom. But—and in this darkest of moments he clung to the thought desperately—but what had Ekar meant by his words, "a most important matter?" What was it that the Black commander-in-chief wanted to know.

As a safeguard against his brain going completely haywire he savagely concentrated on trying to answer that question. A million-and-one different reasons came to him, but none fitted in correctly.

And he was still pondering the question when eventually his bound wrists were jerked backward and he was pulled up to an abrupt halt. They had traversed the full length of the hill ridge and down the far slope. A few feet ahead was a logging road, and hidden under the trees beyond, an armored car.

117

A hand gripped Dusty's arm—it was one of the Black's—and in silence he was led over to the car and pushed into the rear seat. A moment later, Biff Bolton was shoved in beside him. Then, a twisted smile on his lips, Ekar got in and sat between them. Two of the soldiers got into the front seat. The other two saluted smartly, about-faced and marched away. Then gears meshed softly, and the car started forward.

Ekar leaned slightly toward Dusty.

"Sorry to keep you tied up, captain," he said, almost apologetically, "but, I know your record for doing the unexpected, and I cannot afford to take chances. The wrath of my commander is not exactly pleasant entertainment."

Dusty grinned.

"Yeah, the Hawk used to be that way, too," he grunted. "Scared stiff of him!"

The verbal barb struck home. Ekar's placid composure fell away instantly. He stiffened rigid and his eyes went agate behind narrowed lids. A flat, deadly quality came into his voice.

"Fear is an unknown quality to me, captain. We shall see what effect it has upon you!"

With that the Black snapped his head front and said no more. The action was mutual as far as Dusty was concerned. Though his cramped position made his bound wrists feel as though they were encircled by red hot wires, he gave no outward sign. He simply clenched his teeth and stared dully at the road ahead.

It twisted in and out among the low hills. But presently it merged onto a flat stretch of ground. The Black behind the wheel increased the speed and the car tore over shrub ground as though it were a state highway. Several encampments of Black Invader troops flashed by but the car didn't once slacken speed. Whenever anything movable blocked his path the driver simply clamped down on the siren button and plowed right on through.

Eventually, though, the outlying sections of Shoal Harbor loomed up ahead, and the dirt road they had been traveling for the last fifteen minutes became a broad street that led through the heart of the town. Rough shacks became houses, and houses became public buildings. But there was no sign of the native populace. Only Black Invaders were to be seen—hundreds of them, jamming both sidewalks and even spilling out into the streets at several intersections. They waved their arms and shouted hoarsely as the armored car raced past.

Beside him, Dusty could almost feel Ekar swelling with bursting pride. Like a conquering hero he bowed to the left and right, even shouted back to some. The triumphal return of the great! And the less great were paying homage. That they had long expected this moment was proven by the crowds of soldiers and officers jamming both sides of the streets.

Savagely Dusty forced himself to keep his eyes straight ahead and his face expressionless. Damned if he'd give these rats anything additional to crow about. But his heart was heavy with bitter chagrin, and the blood burned through his veins like liquid fire.

Out of the corner of his eye he caught a glimpse of Biff Bolton, seated on the other side of Ekar. The big pilot's face was also expressionless. But there was a certain tightness about the jaws, and his lips were compressed in a thin flat line.

DOWN THE entire length of the street went the car, right down to the harbor water-front where destroyer and submarine flotillas swung lazily at anchor. Then the driver swung the car back, turned off into a side street and headed toward a huge marble and granite building that dominated a large square at the end. In front of it the car stopped. Here too, were crowds of Black troops and like flood waters they swept forward and completely hemmed in the car. Black Invader jargon shook the air.

Then Ekar stood up and raised his right hand. Instantly the silence of a tomb settled over the milling horde. Words that Dusty did not understand spilled from the man's lips. When they stopped, thousands of throats roared out obvious acclaim. Then Ekar spoke again and the mass, fronting the steps leading up to the marble and granite building, fell back to either side, leaving a wide passageway up the steps.

Kicking Dusty's feet out of his way, Ekar climbed down from the car and turned. His lips were curved back in a smile, but his cheeks twitched with excitement, and his eyes were virtually on fire.

"Step down!" he ordered. "Both of you!"

Dusty hesitated as a sense of savage stubbornness gripped him. Then, on impulse, he climbed down. Biff Bolton followed him, and stood grim-faced and silent at his side. Dusty swayed close, touched his shoulder with his own.

"Sorry, buzzard!" he got out quietly.

The big fellow looked at him, actually grinned.

"Nothing to be sorry about, skipper," he grunted. "These bums are giving me a great kick. Betcha we'll be telling our grandchildren about this some day!"

Dusty felt ashamed of his own thoughts. And he'd always believed he could take it? Hell, he couldn't even hold a candle to chaps like Biff!

He started to speak, but didn't. Ekar gave them both a shove, and caught up the trailing lines.

"March!" he barked in his peculiar voice. "Straight up the steps!"

Shoulder to shoulder, like captive Christians of early Roman days, Dusty and Biff started up the long flight of wide stone steps. With every step the thunderous, savage roar of the milling multitude crashed against their ear-drums.

When they reached the top, two Black guards swung open massive doors. Beyond was a long stone floored corridor. Halfway down the right side it was intersected by another corridor that ran off at right angles.

At every ten paces stood an armed guard who saluted with his rifle as Ekar herded the two Yanks past. At the end of the intersecting corridor the Black jerked them to a halt in front of steel- and bronze-embossed doors. Upon these doors he pounded his first, and shouted in his native tongue.

A second later the doors swung noiselessly inward, revealing a large, domed-ceiling room. In the center stood a circular cage-like affair, some five feet high and opened at the top. To the left and facing it were three rows of what could almost be church choir stalls. Three more faced it on the right. Between them, but located on the third side, was a raised dais upon which was a massive, high-backed chair of beautifully carved walnut, inlaid with a mosaic design of highly polished teakwood.

One glimpse of it all and then Dusty was shoved roughly forward. He stumbled, but caught himself in time. Two Black guards appeared out of nowhere and seized hold of him and Biff. The wired cord was stripped from their wrists, and then they were led into the cage-like enclosure.

It was then that Dusty saw the sets of shackles clamped to upright supports. Into a pair his hands were thrust. Together they clicked shut, and he found himself facing the raised dais. Three feet to his left, stood Biff Bolton, also shackled to the uprights. As their eyes met, Dusty flashed him a grin. Then he concentrated on a more detailed survey of the room.

THAT THE building had once served as the local seat of government he had already surmised. And this room, where he was now held a helpless prisoner, had undoubtedly been the assembly room where the town law-makers convened.

But now it was obviously the tribunal room of a savage horde of world destroyers—perhaps even it was Fire-Eyes' permanent headquarters. That massive chair on the raised dais was his seat of honor, was unquestionable. It was big enough to hold two ordinary Blacks. The choir stalls were where his lesser lights sat and aided him in meting out punishment to the condemned—and God help the condemned!

"Boy, I could sure do with a steak about now!"

The inane statement from Biff Bolton's lips was so totally

unexpected and so totally out of keeping with the situation, that Dusty roared with laughter in spite of himself.

"Me, too, kid!" he yelled. "And all smothered with mushrooms and—"

"Silence, dogs!"

Ekar had stepped around in front of them, and slitted eyes burned upward into their faces.

"You are about to meet the all-highest!" he got out harshly. "Prisoners will do well not to laugh. It does not make for mercy."

"And that's another laugh!" Dusty rapped down at him. "Mercy from whom—you tramps? Go to hell, will you?"

Ekar's hand started up toward the chains suspended from the shackles clamped about Dusty's wrists. But as though a sudden thought deterred him, he dropped his hand back to his side.

"There will be plenty of time to pay my personal respects to you, Captain Ayres!" he said in a low, almost toneless voice.

A burning retort was on Dusty's lips, but he didn't say it. For at that moment a bell clanged loudly and a door behind the dais opened. Bodies rigid, cruel eyes fixed straight ahead, twenty odd Black officers filed slowly into the room. Half of them turned sharp left and seated themselves in the stalls.

The other half turned sharp right and took their places in the opposite stalls. There was not a sound save for the faint scuffling of their feet on the floor. Arms folded across their chests they sat like so many wooden Indians, eyes still fixed steadfastly in front of them.

Then the bell clanged a second time. Ekar moved swiftly to

a place beside the dais, raised his right hand, and bellowed out something. It was undoubtedly an announcement, for every Black in the stalls leaped to his feet and executed the peculiar Black Invader salute—right forearm raised so that the hand was on a line with the shoulder, the palm facing front.

Three seconds ticked past and then the open doorway was virtually filled with the giant figure of Fire-Eyes. Dusty stared at him, fascinated in spite of himself. The Invader commander was garbed the same as when Dusty had seen him face to face on two other occasions. He wore the same close-fitting, coarse black uniform, free of insignia except the braided green gold on the shoulder straps. Black gauntlets covered his hands. Over his face, the same green mask with its two slits behind which blazed two orbs of flickering flame. And to top all, the same close-fitting skull-cap that draped down over the nape of his neck.

For an instant the mysterious figure paused, slowly turned his head from left to right, and swept the entire gathering with those terrible eyes. Then he took two long strides forward, stepped up on the dais, and relaxed in the big chair.

As he seated himself, a booming yell burst out. A motion of Fire-Eyes' gauntleted hand and it subsided instantly, and all, save Ekar, became seated once more. Ekar, however, stepped close to the Black commander and spoke in a low voice that came to Dusty as only a murmur. Then as Fire-Eyes nodded again, the Black pilot stepped back and turned; facing the prisoners' cage.

"Your luck has failed you at last, Captain Ayres!"

The voice of Fire-Eyes boomed out and crashed against all four walls. Dusty forced himself to look straight into those flaming orbs.

"Perhaps," he said, tight-lipped. "So what?"

The Black's hands balled into massive fist.

"Speak when not asked to, captain," he thundered, "and it will be your last act in life!"

Dusty grinned, waited. Fire-Eyes continued a few moments later.

"When our great ace went to his glorious reward, Captain Ayres, your own life on this earth was doomed. But I tire of waging war—I have no wish to reduce your country to smouldering ruins. It could then be of no possible use to us. And as it stands now, it is the richest country in the world. But—"

The Black cut himself off short, leaned forward on one arm.

"But," he repeated, "if I am forced to such measures, I shall carry them out to the last death. You are a great hero in your country, but you are only one man. However, for the present, the fate of your country rests with you. As a reward for a small service to us, I give you my word that you will simply be a prisoner until hostilities have ceased. A prisoner—not a dead man, Captain Ayres!"

The Black commander paused for obvious emphasis. Dusty couldn't keep the words on his tongue.

"Thanks, but I'm not interested."

"Perhaps we can induce you to become interested!" Fire-Eyes boomed back at him. "Your aeronautical design expert—one Major Pratt—has perfected a design far in advance of anything now in existence. It was our desire to destroy it for all time. But we did not move fast enough.

"The three completed planes left Cleveland too soon. You flew one, this other American flew the other. Lieutenant Brooks flew the third. Two of those planes are now at Washington under heavy guard. If forced to, we can destroy them, and your national capital as well. But we are interested in procuring one of the planes for study and improvement by our own aeronautical experts. Two are beyond reach. But the third, the one Lieutenant Brooks is now flying—that one we can get!"

Dusty laughed in his face.

"Yeah?" he grated. "Try and get it!"

A low growl slid from lip to lip, but Fire-Eyes didn't even move.

"You will get it for us, Captain Ayres!" he boomed. "You will radio your comrade to come to your assistance at a certain spot we shall name. There will be no bloodshed—you have my word on that. The three of you will be simply prisoners. More than that, honored guests, though a trifle unwilling guests, perhaps. Is that not all quite simple, captain?

"Your country will be saved from complete destruction. Your own life, and those of your two comrades will be spared—to say nothing of your other countrymen. And you will spend the rest of the war as a respected and honored prisoner.

"All that in return for but a short radio message. Incidentally, it will be arranged so that Lieutenant Brooks will never know—just in case that phase of it bothers you."

The Black commander turned his head toward his puppets

seated in the stalls. As one man they all nodded their bullet-shaped heads in a gesture of complete approval.

DUSTY CLENCHED his fists, and the sharp edges of the shackles bit into his wrists. But he didn't even feel the pain. He was too overcome with blind rage to feel anything except seething contempt and withering scorn for the Black commander-in-chief.

Just a simple radio message to Curly, eh? Just sell out his pal, like that? And the reward would be all hotsy-totsy! The word of Fire-Eyes! Hell, the murdering devil didn't even know the meaning of the word honor! He couldn't even be honest with himself—the damn baby-killer! Why even a fool could see through his words. For the sake of capturing one plane intact— just one plane out of thousands—he agreed to restrain the war methods of his vultures and slaughtering hordes? Nuts!

"You agree, Captain Ayres?"

Dusty could almost feel Biff Bolton's eyes upon him. But he only looked straight at Fire-Eyes.

"Agree?" he echoed harshly. "You're slipping, Fire-Eyes! You know damn well that I wouldn't even agree to give you a button off my tunic! Agree? Hell, go take an aspirin! You need it!"

The Black commander still sat motionless. But Ekar let out a bellow of rage, and leaped toward the prisoners' cage. He grabbed the dangled shackle chains and jerked down savagely. Dusty thought that his two wrists had been broken, and he bit down hard on his lower lip to kill the groan of pain struggling to get free.

"Respect from you, or you'll be torn limb from limb!"

Dusty forced himself to stare down into the twisted upturned features; forced the words out between pain-clenched teeth.

"Just two minutes alone with you, rat! That's a minute more than I'd need!"

Ekar raised his hands for the chains again, but stopped short as Fire-Eyes spoke.

"AGREE? YOU KNOW DAMN WELL I WOULDN'T!"

"Once have I caused you to agree with me, captain. And what I have done once, I can do twice!"

Having said that in Dusty's tongue, the Black commander roared out more in his own language and stood up.

Instantly things began to happen fast, and the next thing

Dusty realized, he and Biff were jammed in between two cruel-faced guards in the rear seat of a car. Ekar sat in front with the driver who was sending the car racing through the streets of Shoal Harbor.

Eventually it roared onto an airdrome on the outskirts of the town and came to a sudden stop in front of a low stone-roofed building. A single glimpse of the towering antenna mast was sufficient for Dusty. He drew his lips back in a tight smile.

"Just let them try and make me!" he grated to himself. "Just let them try!"

But a moment later some of his grim determination faded away, and his heart started thumping against his ribs. Leaving one guard to cover him, the other guard pulled Biff Bolton unceremoniously from the back seat of the car and started marching him toward a side door in the radio broadcasting building.

The big pilot, though his wrists had been bound, resisted physically.

"Say!" he growled. "Not so rough, mug!"

As he spoke, he pivoted and brought up one knee. It caught the Black guard square in the pit of the stomach. Air whistled through his teeth and he promptly folded up like an old army cot.

Instantly two other guards leapt upon Biff. The big pilot did his best with his feet. But it was not enough. A rifle butt crashed down on his skull and he sank to the ground. Panting from the exertion the two Blacks picked him up, as they would a dead log, and lugged him through the door.

"Nothing compared with his ultimate reward!"

Dusty, who had been helplessly watching Biff's foolhardy efforts, jerked his eyes around to Ekar's face. The Black had resumed his almost pleasant smile.

"I'm beginning to feel almost sorry for you, tramp!" Dusty clipped out. "Yup, almost sorry!"

Ekar's brows drew together in a sharp frown of perplexity. The remark had sailed clean over his head. He started to speak, but his words were drowned out by the ungodly wail of half a dozen sirens. A moment later a virtual caravan of armored Black Invader cars brake-screamed to a stop in front of the radio building. Fire-eyes was seated in the rear seat of the lead car, practically filling it all by himself.

A couple of flunkies jumped out of the front seat and opened the door. Out stepped the Black commander, passing through the front door of the radio building without so much as giving Dusty a single glance. But he must have made some kind of a signal, for two guards grabbed hold of Dusty, hauled him out of the car, and marched him in in the wake of Fire-Eyes.

The interior was the same as that of any powerful station. Its only difference from any one of hundreds of American stations was that it contained Black Invaders.

SUCH WAS Dusty's cockeyed thought as the guards led him over to a wall transmitting panel and slammed him down in a chair. Both arms, like Biff's were lashed behind his back, numb with pain from shoulder-sockets to finger-tips. His head was whirling and everything was swimming in a sea of blurred red. But with savage grimness he maintained a scornful grin on his lips. Force him to send word to Curly? He'd see the lot of them boiling in hell, first!

"Ready, captain! Maximum volume is on, and it is set on the emergency wave-length. Speak into that transmitter in front of you! He will land at the abandoned field twenty miles south of here."

Dusty glanced up at Fire-Eyes, towering at his side.

"Are you deaf as well as dumb?" he snapped. "You heard what I said to you!"

A gauntleted hand dropped on his shoulder, and steel fingers contracted ruthlessly. Dusty's shoulder felt like bone and flesh pulp, and it was all he could do to refrain from screaming. Then the contraction abated and the Black boomed out words anew.

"I made you talk once, captain, and I can do it twice. You have the courage for pain—for yourself. But you do not have the courage to stand the pain of others. Look—to your left!"

As the command roared out, Dusty instinctively obeyed. He sucked in his breath in a gasp.

A side door had been flung open, revealing a small connecting room. It was the power room for the station. That Dusty saw and realized in a glance. What jerked the gasp from his lips was the sight of Biff Bolton bound helpless on a sort of operating table.

The big pilot had been stripped bare from the waist up. An iron hoop was clamped across his heavy chest. His big hairy arms were shackled to the side of the table, as were his legs also. And a sort of vise arrangement made it impossible for him to even move his head from side to side. Beyond him stood a Black in the white garments of a medical surgeon. In one rubber gloved hand he held a shiny instrument somewhat like an icepick in shape. And in the other he held a long pair of forceps.

"Damn you, he has nothing to do with this!"

Dusty's mad cry was spontaneous. Rolling laughter thundered out from behind the green mask.

"On the contrary, he has everything to do with this, Captain Ayres! Send out that message and he will be released from his present position, instantly. Refuse, and the good surgeon will transform him into a babbling maniac—useful to no one. And a very painful operation too, so the good surgeon tells me."

Dusty's heart froze. Cold sweat oozed out on his forehead and trickled down into his eyes. He fought desperately for a means of gaining time—time in which to think. Curly or Biff? Curly or Biff? Curly or Biff?

The two names pounded and pounded around in his swimming brain. He gasped out the words.

"Wait, damn you, wait! I don't know where Brooks is. I haven't seen him since last night. He may not be where he can receive my call. I—"

"One is a lie, captain!" Fire-Eyes cut in on him. "We know that you saw him while flying up here. Perhaps you do not know where he is now—but we do! Three times he has been sighted near this area, and three times he has escaped. He is still in the air. Speak into that transmitter, now!"

"Don't, skipper!" Biff Bolton's voice suddenly roared out. "The hell with them!"

The last was finished by a groan of pain that sliced through

133

Dusty heart like a knife. Through blurred red he saw the Black surgeon trace a bleeding line across Biff's chest. Words clogged in his throat, then came tumbling off his lips like a loosened torrent of water.

"Stop! Stop! Let him go! I'll send the call. I'll send the call, now. Let him go. He—"

Dusty saw Biff's chest muscles quiver as the big pilot strained against the hoop clamp. Then his bellowing voice. "Ayres! Damn you, Ayres! Keep your mouth shut, I tell you! Don't talk! Hear me? Keep your mouth shut!"

The words ringing in his ears, Dusty gritted his teeth and turned toward the transmitter panel. Then he sucked in his breath and bent forward.

"Calling Two-Four-Two! Calling Two-Four-Two! Curly! Check back to me on Two-Four-Two!"

"Damn you Ayres! Don't! You—"

A groan of pain drowned out the last. Dusty jerked his head around and saw the second red line across Bolton's chest.

"Can't help it, Biff!" he choked out. "I can't help it! Forgive me, buzzard!"

"Forgive you?" the other thundered back. "By God, I'll square with you in hell! You wait!"

At that moment a green signal light on the panel blinked and out of the built-in speaker tube came a voice, the sound of which seemed to squeeze Dusty's heart to a senseless pulp.

"Two-Four-Two checking back! Dusty! Where are you? Where are you? Dusty! Curly checking back on Two-Four-Two! Where are you?"

Without having to turn his head, Dusty sensed the tensed excitement that virtually charged the atmosphere of the room. In the small room beyond, Biff Bolton was choking out curses and groans of pain in the same breath.

"Speak now! The abandoned airdrome, twenty miles due south!"

The order that came from behind the green mask was in a deadly whisper. Body rigid, heart standing still in his chest, Dusty opened his lips.

"Curly!" he yelled wildly. "Curly! Emergency! Scram at once. Get word through to H.Q. Ships, planes, everything to NF-Eight! Shoal Harbor—NF-Eight! Emergency! Blast it off the map. Quick! Get word through to H.Q. Ships, planes—"

The booming roar of a thousand enraged bulls crashed against his ear-drums. Then a ball of steel slammed against the side of his head. He had a split second's vision of radio instruments, Black uniforms, windows and doors all spinning around in a crazy circle. Then a flash of brilliant light, a falling curtain of inky darkness—and he knew no more.

CHAPTER 11
TRIPLE TRAP

"GOD, SKIPPER, I'm sorry! I didn't know! Skipper, I didn't know! I thought you were going to do what they told you. Honest, I didn't know!"

Words—panting, choking, sobbing words coming from out

of the midst of a swirling black fog. Over and over again, like the drumming beat of hail stones on the roof.

Desperately Dusty tried to place them, connect them up with something definite as he probed about in a world of swirling darkness. They hammered against his ear-drums, echoed and re-echoed inside his head. Yeah—yeah, he'd heard that voice before, often. But where was he? Why couldn't he see? Everything was so damn black. Maybe he was asleep and dreaming. Must be that. Funny, dreaming that you're asleep. One for the book, that. He'd have to tell Curly and Biff about it. Damn queer—

"Skipper! Hang on! Hang on, old man! You mustn't let go! You mustn't!"

The last made queer crackling sound in Dusty's head. The black mist swirled away into oblivion, and the strained and anxious features of Biff Bolton took its place.

For a moment Dusty gaped wide-eyed at his pal and waited for memory to come back. It returned slowly, bit by bit and then suddenly finished up in a whirlwind rush of meaning. He closed his eyes as though in so doing he might shut out the splitting pain in his head. It didn't help and he opened them again, rubbed his right hand down his cheek.

"God, skipper, but you sure had me scared that time. I thought his wallop had busted your head!"

Dusty's tongue was thick in his mouth.

"Whose? I think it did, anyway."

"That rat, Fire-Eyes!" replied Bolton. "I was just able to catch a glimpse of his fist swinging down. Gosh, skipper—I don't know what to say. The things I said to you—"

"Forget it!" grunted Dusty, screwing up his face in pain. "Had to do it that way. Hell, I couldn't give in to them, even if they—you—me—I mean—"

The last was jumbled up for loss of adequate words to explain himself.

"I know, skipper," Biff said quietly. "You did the only thing you could. You and me didn't count. It was Curly who mattered most."

Dusty was only half listening as Biff blurted out what was supposed to mean that he understood. Dusty let his eyes rove about the room. There wasn't much to see. Three walls, the ceiling, and the floor were of solid stone. The fourth wall was of solid stone also, save for a heavy, steel-barred door. Beyond it, in the passageway outside, a Black guard was pacing slowly up and down. Each time he passed the door he glanced in, and his lips slid back over stained teeth in a leering smile.

"—don't get the idea that you didn't do right. Wouldn't have done any different myself," Bolton went on.

The words filtering into Dusty's head jerked his attention back to the speaker.

"How'd we get here, Biff?" he asked.

Bolton grunted.

"Huh? Why I've just been telling you! Sure, you're all right, skipper?"

"Sorry," grunted Dusty. "Didn't hear you. Yes, I'm all right. What happened?"

"Well, I don't know all of it," began the big pilot. "As I just told you, all hell broke loose. Boy, did those tramps get mad! Thought sure we were both sunk for keeps. Sounded like an earthquake, no less. Anyway, the rumpus lasted for a couple of minutes. Then the big guy, Fire-Eyes, shouted the others down. Must have, because they all shut up. Then he goes on booming out in his lingo for a couple of more minutes. Then out the door he goes. Boy, is my flesh creeping then! That guy in white has his lamps on me—and I sure felt like nothing at all going nowhere."

Bolton paused to swallow and get his breath. But Dusty was impatient.

"Yeah? Then what?"

Biff hunched his shoulders, gestured with both hands.

"Then all the lights went out," he said. "My God—wonder if I fainted? Nope! I'm sure I didn't have this goose egg on my konk!"

The big pilot paused again, put up his hand and gingerly touched a big lump on the side of his head. He winced and quickly lowered his hand.

"And the next thing I know, I'm here in this place. Guess they must have carried us here. Gave me back my clothes, anyway."

It was then that Dusty noticed for the first time that Biff had on his OD shirt and tunic. He gave his pal a keen look.

"Your chest, Biff? O.K.?"

The other shrugged.

"Could feel better, but I'm not kicking. The bum just slit the skin a bit. But, skipper, what the hell do we do now?"

Dusty didn't answer. He had been asking himself the same question for the last few minutes. What was there to do?

He glanced through the barred door to the Black guard in the passageway beyond. Biff saw his look and read his thoughts.

"It's locked, skipper," he grunted. "I tried it, and that tramp outside gave me the horse-laugh. I guess we park here awhile, huh?"

Dusty nodded absently.

"Yeah, I guess you're right," he murmured. "But I'd sure like to know why they didn't polish us off. We're not much use to them now. Curly got my message. He'll relay it to Washington H.Q. Horner and Bradley will send—"

HE LET the rest trail off. A second guard had appeared in the hallway outside. He was walking toward the first guard, who at the moment was back to him. Suddenly Dusty's heart looped over inside his chest. There was something about the second guard—the swing of his shoulders as he glided along the passageway—that looked vaguely familiar. Dusty felt Biff stiffen at his side. He shot out his hand and grabbed his pal's arm and squeezed hard. Breathlessly, they watched the drama taking place in the passageway.

The first guard had reached the end of the passageway, and was turning slowly back. Then he saw the second guard. His face went blank for an instant. Then he opened his mouth, started to bring up his rifle. But the second guard was less than two feet from him. A gas-gun in his clenched right hand hissed a thin stream of purple smoke, catching the first guard square in the face. He dropped like a fallen log. But the second guard caught him before he hit the floor, then half turned.

Dusty wanted to shout at the top of his lungs. He knew now. He could clearly see the lean face smeared a dull copperish hue. The disguise wasn't bad, but it didn't fool him for a second. The man was Curly Brooks!

At that very moment Curly turned all the way around, flashed them both a grin, and raised a warning finger. Holding the Black guard clear of the floor, he unhooked a ring of keys fastened to the man's belt. Seconds later he had the correct one fitted in the lock of the cell door. A sharp click and he swung it open. Then he carried the Black into the cell.

"My God, kid! How did you—?"

Curly cut off Dusty's whispered exclamation with a quick gesture.

"Pipe down!" he breathed. "Hell, it's about time I got in on this party! Both of you follow me and save your questions. There's a million of the bums outside!"

All of which didn't mean much to Dusty at the moment. But he didn't stop to figure it all out. Good old Curly had crashed through again—and for the time being his lean pal was leading the parade.

As the three of them started through the door, Dusty, on sudden impulse, bent over and scooped the Black's automatic out of its holster clip. Biff Bolton, seeing his action, bent over and picked up the guard's rifle. And then, all of them armed, they started down the passageway with Curly in the lead, Dusty next, and Biff pulling up the rear.

The passageway was perhaps fifty yards long, but to Dusty it seemed fifty miles. At the end was a circular stairway leading up. Leading up to where? The question repeated itself over and over again in his head as he moved forward. Perhaps Curly knew. How the devil did he get in in the first place?

Dusty didn't have time to decide. Curly Brooks stopped abruptly at the foot of the stairs, turned toward them and motioned them closer with a jerk of his head. Silently, they obeyed.

"Here's the picture," he breathed softly. "These stairs lead up to the main field office that's connected to one of the hangars. Most of the bums are over on the other side of the field. At least they were when I sneaked in. Now, we've got to chance it. I think they mean to quit the field. They think I relayed your call."

Dusty gasped.

"My God, didn't you?"

Curly shook his head.

"Couldn't without giving my position away. I'd shaken them off and was sliding in to a landing when your message came through. Another couple of minutes and I wouldn't have heard it."

"But, your ship, kid?" insisted Dusty. "You don't understand. That's what all the fuss is about. Ours are at Washington. So they're trying to get yours."

"That's what I figured," Curly cut in. "Hell, they caught me a couple of times—but didn't open fire, see? Just ordered me to land. Well, I knew then what they were up to. So I just gave them a run for their money and eventually gave them the slip. The crate's about twenty miles north of here. I can pick it up later—after you two lads get away."

"Wait a minute!" Dusty exclaimed. "We've still got a job to do, Curly. They've got something here. We can't pull out now. But how'd you get here? How'd you find us?"

Brooks tapped his gas-gun.

"Walked and used this," he said grimly. "Caught one of them napping and took his uniform. Had to kill three others before I found someone who did know where you were. Took me most of the damn day. My gosh, kid, you'll give me gray hairs, yet. I've been hunting for you ever since I went down last night. But hold it. This is no place to chin. Stick close. I know the ropes."

With that, Curly turned and started up the stairs. Brain racing with a million-and-one different thoughts, Dusty followed him silently, Biff tagging his heels.

At the top, the stairs led off into a large office, and it was then that Dusty realized that illumination below had been only electric light. With a jolt he stared at a window on the far side of the room and saw the waning light of a dying day filtering through. Absently he cheeked it with his watch. The hands showed twenty minutes past four. He and Biff had been in the prison cell for a good eight hours!

Curly's hand gripping his arm jerked him back from his dumbfounded reverie. The lean pilot was pulling him across the room to a small door. In front of it he paused, shifted his gas-gun to his left hand, and took hold of the door knob with his right. He opened it an inch or two to expose the murky interior of an unlighted hangar.

Leaning over his pal's shoulder, Dusty could see the dim outlines of several planes of various types. And then, suddenly he realized the truth. The place was not an active plane hangar but a combination hangar and general store-shed. Hence, no light, and the fact that it appeared to be deserted.

"Swell, kid!" he breathed at Curly. "That cabin ship, over to the left. We can park there, and dope something out."

"Like hell!" Brooks hissed back. "Our luck can't hold forever I They'll soon discover that you're gone. There's a ship out in front. You and Biff swipe it and get going. And I'll—"

Dusty shut him off by pushing him gently but firmly through the door. Then with a nod at Biff, he led the way around a couple of Black Darts and over to a cabin plane near the rear wall of the big shed. Jerking open the door he motioned his two friends inside. Curly hesitated, scowled, then got in without a word. Dusty was the last and he closed the cabin door quietly behind him.

As they all squatted on the floor, well below the cabin windows, Dusty leaned forward and touched Curly's arm.

"Maybe you're right," he said softly, "but we've got to risk it. Everything's haywire and we'd just be going in circles. First let me outline it from the beginnings—"

"Save it, Dusty," Curly cut in. "I know the story. I saw General

Horner. He told me about Jack and about your plan to meet this Ekar at Maine-Seven."

He stopped short as Dusty gripped his arm.

"Before that, Curly. Last night. What happened to you? We thought you had—"

"So did I. Damn near crashed. That purple stuff damn near hit me. Not quite, though. But it did make the engine quit, and the radio too. Managed to get down O.K. But it took me three hours to fix the ship. Then I headed for our field—but the whole squadron had gone. So I high-balled for Washington.

"General Horner was on the field—so were your two ships. Horner didn't know what had become of you. When he told me the story, I figured that you'd taken another ship. So I hit out for Maine-Seven, saw the radio ships, and scrapped their escort. I headed south again, and met you. God, I damn near let drive at you. Where'd you get that crate?"

In a few short sentences Dusty told how Biff had rescued him. Curly grinned at the big pilot.

"A job, isn't it, Biff, getting this guy out of jams?"

"Nuts!" Dusty grunted. "Go on with your story. Just how in hell did you find us?"

Curly shrugged.

"Simply followed you, at high altitude. Saw the Blacks below me, tagging you through the clouds. Knew then, that they wanted to take you alive.

"After awhile they all landed. That meant, of course, that you were down, too. It also meant that it was time for me to get down, if I was going to be of any help. So I flew north and came in that way.

"They won't find the ship in a month of Sundays. Now for the love of Mike, Dusty, you and Biff get the hell out of here. With this get-up I'll be able to mosey back to my crate. In fact, I'll even be kind-hearted enough to fly escort for you on the way back. It'll be dark soon, and it'll be a cinch for us. Then later we can come back with the gang and teach these bums a lesson."

DUSTY SMILED in spite of himself. Curly's matter-of-fact enthusiasm was certainly contagious, but it was also just a bit haywire, considering the corner they were in.

True, the lean pilot had performed a miracle. Knowing only half the story, he had nevertheless plowed right through and saved them both. He'd succeeded where Dusty and Biff, with all their planning, had failed miserably. But, stepping out of the picture might not be so simple. And there was one thing that must delay the stepping.

The mystery was still far from solved. Here they were at NF-Eight, the very center of the whole hellish business, if Jack Horner was right. Trying to escape was simply throwing away what little advantage they had gained.

"You still don't get the angle, Curly!" Dusty said suddenly. "We've got to trip up this Ekar bum. Wipe him out, and this damn place along with him. Now by checking what little we've found out, this is what I figure. He has a flock of radio-controlled ships that carry some new chemical discovery of his instead of bombs. He practically admitted it to Biff and myself. We know what the hellish stuff will do. We've got to fight him with his own weapons, see?"

Curly shook his head doggedly.

"Nope. What do you mean?"

"Bait," said Dusty bluntly. "They want your ship—at least one of the three. And they think getting yours is their best bet. To get it, I believe they're willing to wait. That's our break. The crate can fly rings around anything they've got. And—well, kid, I hate like hell to mention it, but—"

"I get it," nodded Curly. "You want me to tease them from the air while you go to work on the ground?"

"Right," said Dusty. "It'll be dark soon. Then you can get back to the ship. Once you're in the air, and they know it, they'll forget about Biff and me. And we'll—"

"But I said awhile ago that I think they're going to quit this field!" Curly blurted out. "Hell, they don't know that I didn't relay the order through. And besides, once they find that you've escaped, they'll be swarming all over the place."

"Exactly the reason why you should get going," Dusty came right back. "Once they know your ship is still around, and that Biff and I have lit out, that'll be two things to bother them!"

Curly was still stubborn. "It just doesn't listen right," he said. Then to Bolton, "What about you, Biff?" The big pilot doing all the listening shrugged and screwed up his face.

"The skipper's right in saying that the three of us lighting out now wouldn't get us much," he grunted. "Personally, I'd like to stick and smack these mugs as long as I can."

Curly sucked in a deep breath, let it but in a long sigh.

"Okay then,"—he said. "If it's your party, then it's your party. I suppose I'll have to come back and pull you both out later."

Dusty cut him off short with a vigorous shake of his head.

"Nix!" he said. "If Biff and I pull I flop—and you'll be able to tell—high-tail south and relay the message through his time. It'll be the only thing left to do!"

The meaning behind Dusty's words was not lost on Curly. He knew perfectly well that a flop would mean that his two pals had died. He opened his mouth to speak—but no words came out. At that instant the eerie wail of a siren just outside the hangar blasted the stillness. Rigid, the three of them looked at each other. There was no need for words. They knew without asking, that the escape of Dusty and Biff had been discovered. And also that any chance of Curly breaking through the cordon of Black troops that would be soon flung about the field, was gone for good.

"Hell!"

The one word hissed off Dusty's lips, but the very tone of it emphasized all the bitterness and helpless chagrin that surged up within him.

CHAPTER 12
FLAMING BLOCKADE

FOR PERHAPS three full minutes they sat crouched on the floor of the cabin plane listening with pounding hearts to the wailing siren outside. Then Dusty shifted his position and moved toward the door.

147

Curly's hand stopped him and the expression on his pal's face asked the unspoken question. Dusty simply grinned and motioned for him to stay right where he was and for Biff to do likewise.

"Maybe it's a break after all!" he whispered. "I've got to see. Stick here."

Ignoring them further, Dusty climbed out through the door, listened motionless for a couple of seconds to the siren blaring its nerve-chilling note, and to the shouting voices that it practically drowned out, and then moved stealthily toward the front of the shed.

The two massive doors were shut, but near the bottom, on a level with the height of a man's eye, were two small windows. Dusty made straight for the nearest one, flattened himself against the door, and cautiously looked out.

At first he saw nothing but a stretch of level ground over which groups of shadowy figures were moving swiftly. But a moment later he noted things in detail. To his left was a stone-roofed building that he recognized instantly—the radio building. Beyond it was a semi-circle of hangars that extended clear around to the other side of the field. In front of the hangars nearest him were Black Darts and several small, fast cabin observation ships. But beyond them was a long line of egg-snouted twin-engine monoplanes. One look at them was sufficient—they were radio-controlled planes. The ones, possibly, that Curly had seen at Maine-Seven.

He started to look to the right, but jerked his eyes back to the radio-controlled planes again. The ship at the far end was totally different from the others. The light was poor, but he was still able to see certain features that brought a puzzled frown to his brows.

It was a monoplane, and like the radio ships, had twin out-board engines cowled into the leading edge of the thick wing. But there the likeness stopped. For one thing its snout seemed to be a double-deck affair. The top was obviously the pilot's compartment. But directly below there was a second compart-ment that had three oblong windows—one on either side and the third forming the curved part of the nose.

Another difference was the rear part of the fuselage—there wasn't any. That is to say, the fuselage ended with the leading edge of the wing. And from there, back to the tail section, were two solid I-beam outrigger booms that faired into the double tailplane, fins, elevators and rudders. The landing gear, as in the case of the radio planes, was of the conventional retractable type—mounted directly under the engines, and folding inward up into the wing.

Fascinated by the sight of the strange craft, he stood staring at it when suddenly a figure ran past outside, not three feet from the window against which his face was pressed. Instant-ly, he dropped and crouched holding his breath, expecting to hear the pounding footsteps pause and come back. But they didn't, and he cautiously straightened up, This time he looked to the right.

More hangars and more planes, mostly of the small cabin type. Their props, however, were ticking over, and he could see black uniformed pilots climbing in through the cabin doors.

Farther back on the tarmac several armored cars, each one full of troops, were getting under way. In snake-like order they rolled off and disappeared from view around the corner of the last hangar.

Dusty gave them but a glance and snapped his eyes back to the planes. The distance was a little under a hundred yards—a hundred yards that led right past the field's main office and prison block where he and Biff had been.

Suddenly a faint noise behind him made him whirl. Curly and Biff were right there, faces aglow with eager questioning.

"What the hell? We've got to do something, kid!"

Curly's words were almost less than a whisper. Dusty flung him a hard look, nodded grimly.

"Right!" he hissed. "Peel off that uniform. I've got an idea. Snap it up."

"Say, listen—!"

"Off, Curly, off!"

The lean pilot hesitated the fraction of a second, then started stripping off the Black uniform, revealing his own underneath. Silently Dusty took each piece and climbed into it. The fit was worse than it had been on Curly. But there was no time to be choosey. He jammed the skull cap down over his head, then signaled them close.

"Keep your eyes open for the first ship that taxies this way. When it gets in front, come running like hell!"

Brooks cursed and looked at Dusty. "You're mad, Dusty, plumb mad! You'd never make it! My God, man, don't you know they're looking for you?"

Dusty silenced him with a look.

"They're looking for two guys, get it?" he snapped. "So one guy, right with them, won't be noticed. Hell, they're running in circles. No time like the present. Oh yeah—get a chute pack out of one of these ships and put it on. See you later."

Curly's hand clutched at him, but Dusty shook his head and turned toward the doors. Taking a final look outside he eased the right door open no more than a foot or so and squeezed through. Then, head down to shield his face as much as possible, he ran brazenly toward the right.

As he came abreast of the main office four Black officer pilots bounded down the steps and for a moment his heart stood still. But they didn't even give him a glance. They too turned sharp right and ran toward the line of cabin planes with props ticking over. Dusty grinned tightly, dropped in some ten or fifteen yards behind, and kept right on running.

The tarmac, when he reached it was virtually alive with excited Blacks. For an instant he thought he heard the harsh voice of Ekar. But he wasn't sure and he didn't dare pause to look around. Time for that later, maybe. The job now was to carry through with the insane, yet only, plan that had popped into his head. Crazy, sure? But what the hell—it was a crazy war, wasn't it?

Snatches of thought skipping through his head, he ran boldly past group after group of Blacks and thanked Providence for the dim murky light of early evening. But as he passed each ship he darted a snap glance at its cabin. The first five had a pilot in the seat. So did the second five, and the third. Little fingers of doubt itched at his heart strings, and the back of his mouth and throat went dry.

AND THEN, almost as he was about to run past it, he came upon one plane into which the pilot was actually climbing. In the split second allowed, Dusty half turned and swept everything, in one flashing glance. The nearest Black was twenty yards away, in his ship and bending intently over the controls. It was now or never.

Swerving, Dusty leapt toward the open door, now filled with the Black pilot's figure. As he crashed into the small of the man's back sending him spinning headlong on the cabin floor, Dusty shot out his free hand. In that free hand he held the automatic he had taken from the prison guard. Its barrel made dull thudding sound on the pilot's skull, and the man went limp and motionless.

In virtually a continued movement, Dusty rose up to his hands and knees, reached back and pulled the cabin door shut, and then darted forward and dropped into the control seat. Not once did he bother to look back at the Black pilot crumpled in a heap on the floor. He didn't have to. He'd put a hundred and eighty-five pounds behind the blow of that gun barrel, and he knew it.

Quickly settling himself in the seat he revved up the engine a bit, snapped a glance at the instruments, found everything O.K., and sat waiting grimly. The ticklish part of it all was yet to come. He didn't dare be the first to taxi out. He'd be noticed too much. His only hope lay in waiting for at least a couple of them to taxi out before he did. Then it would be relatively easy.

DUSTY LEAPED TOWARD THE OPEN CABIN DOOR

The take-off runway ran directly in front of him past the store hangar where Curly and Biff waited. He'd take it slow at the start—make it look as though he were coddling his engine.

But with each passing second his heartbeat went up a couple of notches. Hell's bells! What were the boobs waiting for? Weren't they ever going to get into the air? My God—!

The last he drowned out in a gulp of relief. A plane on his right had taxied out and was slowly trundling down the runway. As it rolled past he caught a glimpse of the streamers fastened to the trailing edge of the wings, understood, and peered hard to see the figure crouched over the stick.

But in the dim light, the figure was only a blur. O.K., swell! All the more chance of him not being spotted and suspected. Two more and then he'd get going!

A wait! Was it one minute or a hundred years? And then a second and a third plane rolled out and started down the runway.

"Oke! Here we go—stick with us, Lady Luck, stick with us!"

Breathing out the words softly, Dusty released the wheel brakes, goosed the engine a bit and let the plane move forward. The other ships were already thundering across the field and swinging up into a twilight sky. The instant he reached the runway, he braked the left wheel and swung the plane around parallel to the tarmac. Easing off the brake he fed just enough hop to the engine to make the plane move forward at average taxi speed.

Seventy-five yards to the store hangar!

Forty yards to go! Now!

Two figures, head and shoulders bent forward, came streaking out of the store hangar. They seemed to be virtually hugging the ground. Steeling himself, Dusty braked hard, then released instantly and let the plane roll slowly.

Out the corner of his eye he saw the cabin door jerk outward, and the body of a man catapult inside, trip over the crumpled Black pilot and go sprawling. And a split second later a second body followed the first in—but not all the way. Just the head and shoulders were inside the cabin.

In a sweeping motion Dusty rammed the throttle wide open, and at the same instant swinging his other hand back, grabbed a handful of slack tunic cloth and jerked with all his might.

"Okay! Let go—I'm in!"

THE HOARSE gasp from Curly's throat came to his ears above the pounding of the engine. He let go, grabbed the stick, shoved it forward, and got the tail up. Seconds later he pulled the plane clear and went arcing up.

Then and then only, he half turned and looked down and back out the side cabin window. A couple of planes were taking off right behind them, but the others were not making any special effort to get into the air. Damned if they hadn't made it—and right under the damn noses of the Blacks, too!

"Hey!" Curly's voice rang out sharply. "Now what's on your mind? You're heading south aren't you?"

"South, my eye!" Dusty grunted, bending over and squinting at the compass. "We're heading north—north to where you left your ship. Then, sweetheart, in case we can't risk a landing, you're going over the side. Until you get that ship back to Washington and under guard, I won't feel right. And—"

155

"Nothing doing!" Brooks growled. "Say, what am I—a bad case of scarlet fever? I tell you they'll never find that ship. I'm sticking! You're up to something, and I'm damned if I'm going to let you leave me out in the rain again! And that's flat!"

Dusty didn't answer for the moment. He was thinking of Curly, and of what he wanted his pal to do. Hell, he'd like nothing better than to have Curly stick and help him with the plan of action that was taking shape in his mind. But, that was just no soap.

The risk of Curly's ship being found was too great. Everything had been revolving about that plane. Why Fire-Eyes and Ekar had let him and Biff live, he didn't know positively. But he could make a damn good guess that in some way it was connected up with getting hold of Curly's plane.

Once they got hold of it, they'd strike—perhaps. But until then they were obviously waiting for something. Those radio-controlled ships and that other queer-looking job had remained on the ground. So what—a screwy mixup all around. But the point was to get Curly headed south in the new job and get word through to Washington H.Q. just in case—just in case he and Biff never went south again.

He heaved a sigh, took his eyes off the sky ahead, and looked at his pal. A sardonic grin was on Curly's lips, and he was nodding slowly.

"Save the lecture, teacher," Curly said. "O.K. I see your point—saw it back there in the hangar. Some one has to get through, and I'm elected. It's my crate and all the rest of it. Now follow the coast up aways. I'll tell you when we get over the place. In the meantime, what's on your mind?"

Dusty grinned, and the look he gave his pal said far more than words possibly could. Like a hundred other times, Curly was damping down on his desire to see a show through, and simply obeying orders. Of such things are real soldiers made!

"I'm curious why those radio ships on the field didn't take off," Dusty said in a low voice. "And with this crate, maybe I can find out. After stubbing my toe a million times I've at last got hold of something worthwhile—it's this crate. I'm in it, and I'm damn sure they don't know it. My plan is to just hang around and see what happens. That's about all."

Curly snorted and stared moodily out the cabin window.

"I don't like it, Dusty!" he mumbled. "Not even a little bit. I—hell, I think that this thing is too damn big for us. I'll step off and take the ship south if you want. But I think you're crazy to stay here."

"Maybe," Dusty said patiently. "But I didn't come up here just for the ride. And I've got a little act to put on with that rat Ekar before I go back. And by the way, keep your shirt on—Biff and I'll be back!"

AS DUSTY stopped talking, heavy silence settled down upon the three of them. Each was too occupied with his own thoughts to speak. Face grim and just a trifle strained, Dusty stared fixedly ahead through the cabin window. In a general way he was following the coast of Newfoundland. Far out over open water he caught an occasional glimpse of a blinker light aboard some

Black warship. But on land there wasn't a single sign of a light. Even Shoal Harbor was shrouded in murky gloom.

A tinge of uneasiness taking hold of him he turned toward Curly once more.

"We must be getting close, kid," he grunted. "You sure you can find the ship?"

"Positive," was the instant answer, "See that jut of land sticking out up ahead? Swing out and follow it back in. You'll spot two hills about a mile inshore. The ship is hidden between them."

As Curly talked, Dusty swung the plane out over the water and then back inshore again so that they were flying directly over a thin jut of land. Darkness was settling down fast now and the ground was an ever-changing panorama of shadows. By peering hard ahead he could just make out two small hills rising up like two sore thumbs from out of a stretch of rugged, shrub covered wilderness. That Curly had made his way from that God forsaken spot twenty miles south to the NF-Eight field seemed almost beyond belief.

While Dusty was musing, the signal light on the radio panel suddenly started blinking. He shot out his free hand, snapped on contact, and spun the wave-length dial. Instantly the cabin speaker unit crackled sound that sent Dusty's blood leaping through his veins. Several Black stations were broadcasting in their secret high speed dot-dash code! By careful adjustment of the dial knob he was able to pick up at least six different signal tones.

At his elbow Curly muttered something, but Dusty didn't

pay any attention. He had snapped on the instrument cowl light and was staring intently at the station directional finder dial, tuning in each station one after the other.

"Hell, they know we're in the air!" came Curly's gasp in Dusty's ear. "Look at that dial—those are planes in the air south of us. Don't you get it? They're forming a blockade in hopes of cutting us off."

Dusty made no comment. A tiny thought was flittering around in the back of his brain. He groped for it desperately. Suddenly, he let out a whoop.

"Got it, got it!" he breathed fiercely. "Hell are we dumb! Should have figured it long ago."

"Certainly!" Curly clipped out. "So what the hell are you talking about?"

"Those ships!" Dusty exclaimed. "Sure they're forming a blockade—keeping contact that way. But the blockade isn't for us! It's for Yank ships they think are heading north! Don't you see? They're afraid that you did relay the message through. They've been waiting to find out for sure. When Biff and I escaped that sent them haywire. So they flung out that advanced patrol. That's why the whole damn place is dark. They plan to get those radio-chemical ships off in secret. Hell—we've just been wasting time."

As he finished the last Dusty swung the ship around in a sharp bank and sent it racing south.

"Where you headed, kid?" asked Curly. "I thought that you—"

"I did," Dusty cut him off. "But your ship will have to wait.

If we don't stop these bums now, it won't matter if they get your crate or not. We're heading back to NF-Eight. Hang on!"

CHAPTER 13
THE BLACK AVENGER

THE SHIP had traveled some five miles or so before Curly suddenly realized that Dusty was climbing the plane at a steep angle. He leaned forward and tapped his pal's shoulder.

"Don't get it at all, Dusty," he said. "However, I'll string along. But what's the program?"

Dusty jerked a thumb backwards without turning.

"Knew that Black would come in handy," he grunted. "I'm going to glide into the field, engine off—land in that far corner. You two get out and I'll put that Black in the seat. Then I punch the engine starter and the ship taxies toward the main office. Once those bums on the ground spot it they'll get curious. Meantime, we fade in the opposite direction and go for the plane at the far end of the line. I got a look at it, and it's my guess it's the control ship. We get it—and those rats will be out of luck. We'll give them some of their own medicine, see?"

"Know the crate you mean," grunted Curly. "Got a quick look at it, but what makes you think—?"

"The double-deck nose," Dusty cut in. "The bottom section's the control room. Dammit—has to be. Oh my God, am I going to be late again?"

Neither of the other two made any attempt to answer the

question. Lips pressed together, faces set with grim determination, they peered out into the shadowy sky. Then presently Dusty cursed softly, reached out and switched off the engine.

"Down we go, fellows!" he grunted. "Remember—you two out as soon as I land. Hug the ground. In case something goes wrong—split up. The end ship on the far side of the field from where we were—one of us has got to get hold of it! Got to—understand? Without it, their damn radio chemical ships are sunk!"

Seconds ticked past, became minutes. Dusty's eyeballs ached and smarted as he peered downward for a single shadowy outline which would give him his exact position.

A faint glow of light ahead and down to his right sent his thoughts flying. Then suddenly the truth came to him and he sucked in his breath in a sharp, rasping gasp. The faint glow was light cast out through the open doors of a hangar. It was dimly silhouetting a row of planes on the tarmac—twin-engined monoplanes with no cabin windows—and their props were slowly ticking over!

A second or two later another open hangar door glowed light, then a third and a fourth until the darkness was marked by a complete half circle of faint, fused light.

"We've got to make it!" Dusty hissed.

As the words hissed off Dusty's lips he swerved the plane to the left and steepened the glide. There was a chance that the low whistle of the plane's wings in the rush of air would be picked up on the ground. But it was a chance that he had to take. Time meant everything now.

If those radio chemical ships and their control plane took off before they landed, God alone knew what part of the United States would feel their hell-death.

This and a million other thoughts tearing through his brain, Dusty guided the plane lower and lower. Fifty feet more and the wheels would touch!

A soft gentle bounce! Instantly Dusty bore down on the wheel brake pedal. The plane quivered, rolled slowly forward in the darkness. Letting go of the stick he hurled himself back out of the seat.

He sensed rather than saw Biff and Curly piling silently out of the cabin door. As his foot struck something soft and yielding he bent over, scooped up the limp figure of the Black pilot and slammed him down into the control seat. A split second later he clamped the stick back against the man with the aid of the safety belt. Then he shot out his hand and opened the throttle to taxi speed.

AT THAT instant a tremendous roar echoed across the night-shadowed airdrome. He knew what it was without even turning to look and his heart looped over. The radio-control ships were being given a last minute rev-up. A muttered prayer on his lips, he thumped down on the electric engine starter and flung himself out through the half open cabin door. Waiting hands in the darkness grabbed him and pulled him flat on the ground and clear of the tail wheel of the plane as its quarter-throttled engine dragged it forward.

"Keep low!" Dusty hissed. "Circle to the left to that end hangar!"

THE BLACK AVENGER

Shadowy movement at his side told him that Biff and Curly had heard and were following his instructions. Running stealthily forward, but bearing to the left, Dusty watched the taxiing plane out of the corner of his eye.

It had picked up considerable speed and was half way across the field and heading straight for the main office. Then suddenly it seemed to hit a bump in the ground, or perhaps its unconscious pilot had somehow slumped against the rudder pedal.

At any rate, the plane swerved sharply to the right and went careening straight for the radio plane on the extreme left of the line—the opposite end to that for which Dusty and his two pals were headed.

It was the break of breaks. With a burst of speed Dusty spurted ahead of the other two, but they were at his heels instantly and running full out.

The double-snouted plane loomed up to his left and he swerved toward it. And at that moment there was a terrific crash of sound at the far end of the tarmac. Brilliant red and purple flame leaped skyward to turn everything into the brilliance of high noon.

What happened, Dusty couldn't tell. The control plane blanketed out the obvious chaos beyond. He could only guess, and know that his guess was correct. The plane with the unconscious Black pilot at the controls had slammed into one of the radio chemical ships, and fuel tanks were exploding.

And then he reached the entrance door of the control plane. In a flash he skidded to a halt, jerked it open and leaped inside.

For an instant the dull glow of a ceiling bulb blurred his vision. He saw a conglomeration of instruments of all description—dials, condensers, rheostats, control levers, batteries, and a hundred different other things. It was a mighty-power plant enclosed in sheet steel and three oblong windows.

Something at the right window moved, spun around. Dusty was still in motion, half stumbling forward, fighting for a grip on something to check his progress. But his eyes were riveted to the moving form at the window.

He saw the twisted snarling face, the cruel blazing eyes and the side of the head that contained no ear. And in the same split second of time he saw Ekar's right hand flash down and up. Red flame spurted, and sound crashed out. A white hot coal nicked the left side of Dusty's neck as he twisted in mid-air and dived forward.

Like a battering ram his body crashed into yielding flesh. Another blaze of red flame, and thundering sound in his ears. Then a yelp of pain, a clang of metal against metal, and a world of spinning stars, moons and comets!

"Hey! Hey, skipper! Take it easy—everything's jake!"

The spinning stars, moons and comets faded into oblivion at the sound of the shouting voice. A moment later Dusty found himself staring stupidly down into the bleeding and pummeled face of Ekar. Biff was pulling him up onto his feet.

The big pilot had a mile-wide grin on his face.

"My God, can you swing a mean fist! But, gosh, that was close, skipper. Sure thought that second slug got you."

His pal's words steadied Dusty, brought memory racing back. He choked out a gasp, looked wildly around.

"Curly! Where's—?"

Biff grabbed him, shook hard.

"Cut it, skipper!" he thundered. "Hold everything! He's where you shouted for him to go—up in the cockpit flying the ship!"

IT WAS only then that Dusty realized that the plane was in motion. Almost vacantly he stared out through one of the oblong windows and down at the ground. Below, a flaming bier etched the NF-Eight field in crimson outline. Swarms of blurred figures were racing about in all directions. The far end hangar was a seething inferno, and the tarmac in front of it was spewing out purple tinted sparks that gave off a paler purple vapor.

Slowly Dusty took his eyes away from the sight, looked down at the crumpled figure of Ekar on the steel floor. He grinned, heaved a big sigh.

"Fools for luck, that's us!" he grunted at Biff. "Got the ship we want and the rat we want, too. Now we'll just bring him around and persuade him to operate these gadgets so that the rest of those radio ships will take off and dive right into the ocean out there. No, by God, we'll have 'em dive into this field!"

He moved toward the Black, yanked him to his feet, and slammed him up against the front of the cabin. Holding him there with one hand, he hand-whipped him across the face with the other.

"Come on, dearie, out of it!" he grated. "I didn't hurt you that much!"

Ekar's eyes opened, gazed glassily around.

"Yup!" Dusty snapped. "It's us! We want to play some more but don't know how. So you're going to show us, see?"

Ekar didn't say anything; just stood motionless. Dusty doubled his free hand into a fist.

"Your pal, the Hawk, didn't like this!" he grated. "How about you?"

With that he chopped his knuckles down the side of Ekar's face. The Black groaned with pain.

"You may kill me!" he snarled. "But your country is doomed!"

As the last word ripped off his tongue he kicked out with his right boot. It crashed against a round glass globe. There was a faint puff of smoke and splintering glass.

"Now, dog, you are helpless—and so am I! Even if I wished to, I could not contact those radio planes below. But others can—and your country is doomed!"

The man finished with a scream that suddenly changed into a torrent of words in his native language. Then Dusty slammed him across the mouth.

"Damn you!" he roared. "One more yip and I'll tear you apart."

Ekar stopped, but he pulled his lips back in a savage smile.

"You are not the only clever one, dog!" he hissed out between his teeth. "Look below!"

Instinctively, Dusty shot his glance downward, made queer noises in his throat. Save for the one plane that was hidden by flames and purple sparks, every one of the radio-controlled chemical ships was thundering across the big field; swinging easily up into the heavens which had now become criss-crossed by a hundred or more power searchlight beams!

CHAPTER 14
THE RADIO DEATH

S TRUCK DUMB by the sight for the moment, Dusty could only gaze stupidly as his brain probed for the answer. A few seconds later he received it from Ekar's own lips. With one hand the Black pointed at the radio panel at his side.

"You understand, captain? First with my foot I destroy the central control tube that contacts the wave-length power adjustments on the radio planes. Good! Neither I nor you can do anything with them. And then—then with my voice I order our main ground station to take over control of the radio bombers, and continue with our original plans.

"I also tell them of my situation. You see, dog, the instrument I smashed does not affect my broadcast set, which I always keep open on the wave-length of our main ground station. Had you used your eyes for other things you would have noticed that signal light burning."

The words fell on Dusty's brain like sledge-hammer blows. The red signal light, as he stared at it for the first time, seemed to ogle at him almost gloatingly. From a long way off he heard more of Ekar's words drumming against his ears.

"Death I have long expected, captain. It is the price we Blacks pay for our greatness. But my pledge to the Black Hawk will have been fulfilled.

"You will die, too. See those searchlights? See how they follow this plane? They will do so until the radio planes have closed in above us. Then—then we become ashes, become nothing! My own chemical mist will engulf us.

"I have so ordered it, and he, the high commander, will respect my last request. My own discovery, captain—my own chemical mist of death. Perhaps we will not even see it. It does not generate its destructive powers until it has mingled with the air, or with the chemicals in the ground. That lapse of time is necessary, you see, else it would destroy its own containers."

The man paused, laughed harshly. Red rage filmed Dusty's eyes. He reached for the man's throat.

"I'm giving you five seconds, rat!" he grated. "Order those ship's to land, or by heaven I'll kill you!"

But the Black only laughed louder.

"Five years, and I would not speak!" he gloated. "Fool, I expect to die! It is the end for me, for you dogs, and for all your countrymen. We expect your air fleets to come up. Do you not recall ordering your swine comrade to relay your message? They should be here some time tonight. They will meet the fleets we have sent out. Our pilots will occupy their time. And while that is taking place, my fool friend, my chemical planes will be directed around them, down to your cities, your airdromes, your army camps—everything the length and breadth of your country will be reduced to ashes."

Dusty's hands itched for the man's throat, but it was no time for personal feelings. Nor was it time to feel any sense of satisfaction that he had guessed right—guessed that the Blacks believed Curly had relayed his message, and were therefore setting up a blockade for the "expected" American aerial armada.

Hell no, there was only time to do something—to get out from under the caravan of death that was even now swinging into position not a mile away!

"Dusty! Biff! We're being boxed! Hang on! I'm going to dive!"

A voice, faint in tone, but unmistakably Curly's! Instinctively, Dusty glanced in back of him, saw the blank steel trapdoor that was shut. The voice hadn't come through there. He glanced above his head, saw only solid steel ceiling. Then the voice of Curly Brooks again.

"Dusty! Biff! Hang on!"

And then he got it! On a hook not two feet from his head, hung a set of earphones. Near them was a speaking tube with wires that led up through the ceiling. Curly's voice was coming out of the earphones!

He moved toward them, but Ekar moved faster, kicked out with his foot and tripped him. Together they went down in a heap. But as they fell Dusty's right fist crashed into the twisted face with its blazing eyes. And in that instant Dusty saw a flash of stark fear and alarm. Then they struck the steel floor.

Ekar lay still, his eyes closed. But Dusty came up like a rubber ball, lunged for the head-phones, jammed them over his head. The Black uniform he wore had become twisted, and snubbed his movements. With a savage curse he ripped it off.

"Damned if I'll die in that!" he husked.

Then he shoved his lips to the speaking tube.

"Curly! Climb, for God's sake. Get above those radio planes! They're controlled from the ground, now. And—"

At that instant, like a blinding flash of light, the real reason for the fear and alarm in Ekar's eyes as he went down, thundered home to Dusty's excitement-whipped brain. God Almighty, the one way out had been staring him in the face ever since he leaped into the plane. It was there right in front of him—a radio-gun fitted to a swivel joint just below the bottom of the oblong window!

A radio gun! The most effective of all weapons at high altitude. And the only one suitable to the control plane of a radio
squadron. Any electrically-operated instrument or powerplant
that came within range of its short-wave beam, was put out of
commission instantly. After that followed fire, as the result of
the intense heat created by the short-wave beam making contact.
Hell's bells yes, the Black Hawk, himself, had used an electric
rifle against him at the time of their final battle.

Yeah, no wonder Ekar had used up so many words. The blasted rat had been stalling for time—hoping against hope that he wouldn't notice the radio gun. But he had, by God! And with no more than seconds to spare, either.

"Dusty! What the hell's wrong? Whatcha stop for?"

Curly's words crackled in his ears. As he answered he swung down the rheostat dial knob on the small panel to the right of the gun. Instantly the steel-walled compartment was filled with a low humming sound, and red liquid in a U-shaped graduated tube started to rise up slowly.

"Curly! Follow my orders for God's sake. Level off! Fly at right angles to that first ship. Snap it up."

THE WORDS were hardly off Dusty's lips when the plane was banked sharp left. Squinting along the sights of the gun, Dusty drew a bead on the left outboard engine of the first radio ship now thundering toward him. A split second later he squeezed the trigger.

Instantly a thread of blue flame spurted from the muzzle of the gun, but trickled down abruptly and was lost. Sight of it, small as it was, dazzled his eyes, made them smart almost unbearably. Through a blinking haze he saw that the red liquid in the U-tube was close to a broad mark. He guessed that it signified the full volume. With a curse he bent over and took a look. The result brought a shaky laugh to his lips. Suspended from the trigger-guard was a pair of metal goggles fitted with green smoke glass.

"No wonder!" he grunted thickly. "Should have figured that!"

With a quick motion he slipped the goggles over his head.

Looking through them seemed to make the oncoming radio ship appear as though it was about to crash into him. In no time at all he lined up the gun again, squeezed the trigger and held it that way. This time the muzzle of the gun spurted a long ribbon of crackling blue light. Across the air space it leapt and seemed to actually smash into the cowled right engine of the radio plane.

Like a giant bird shot in mid-flight, the radio plane heeled over on wing, seemed actually to skid sidewise through the air, then down it went and was gone.

"My God, what's that?"

Curly's voice blasted in Dusty's ear.

"Me!" he howled back. "Left bank—nose up, quick!"

The order was instantly obeyed and Dusty swung his radio gun on a second radio-controlled ship and pulled the trigger. Blue flame spurting out again. And again its darting tip smashing into an engine cowling. But this time the plane flopped over completely on its back, swerved half around and darted forward. Perhaps it traveled fifty yards before it crashed headlong into a third radio plane. The explosion that followed rocked the control plane so much that Dusty was almost flung off his feet.

Cursing, shouting at the top of his voice he clung to the radio gun, held the trigger all the way back, and swung the gun from side to side. And all the time he was dimly conscious of Curly's voice.

What his pal was yelling, he did not know. Nor did he particularly care at the moment.

The entire heavens had become filled with a billion prisms that spun and whirled about in a weird, grotesque pattern of ever-changing colored light.

Not a single hue of the rainbow was missing. Red, orange, yellow, green—all of them, doubled and tripled, losing themselves in each other, and coming into full brilliance again. A sight wondrous as it was horrible. From heaven to earth it slithered and showered down; struck and mushroomed out and came billowing upward.

"God—there—off to the right!"

Curly's roaring voice crashed against Dusty's brain and shook him out of his madman's trance.

"Look where?" he mumbled into the speaking tube.

"To the right!" came the reply. "Down there to the right—the NF-Eight field!"

RIPPING OFF his goggles Dusty pressed his face to the window and looked down. The entire NF-Eight field and surrounding ground was a sea of smoking purple sparks.

It was like a gigantic wave sweeping forward—a wave of pale purple mist with a foaming crest of purple sparks. Over buildings and hangars it swept, consuming them all, as though it were a great steam roller that crushed them into the very bowels of the earth.

A choked gasp tore Dusty's eyes from the sight. Biff Bolton stood wide-eyed beside him. His big right paw was curled about the tunic collar of Ekar, who hung limply, feet and hands trailing on the steel floor.

"God—God, skipper! Didja see them? They all went slamming down together. Radio control must have gone screwy. Lord, it gives me the creeps!"

Dusty grunted but said nothing. He couldn't think of any words to say. Biff was right—radio control had gone screwy.

Plain luck, or the god of right, had sent one of those falling planes crashing into the main ground control station, blasting it to smoking ruins. Control and power cut off, the remaining ships had dropped like rocks, and now the creation of Ekar's war-twisted brain was completing the hell havoc as it burned its deadly self into oblivion.

"Hell!" he snapped. "The job isn't done yet. Curly's ship. We've still got to get it!"

Shooting out his hand he grabbed the speaking tube.

"Curly!" he called. "Head north! We've still got to pick up your ship before we pull out. I'll—"

"For God's sake," the earphones crackled, "have you been taking a nap? If there's anything left on this damn hunk of ground worth flying, including my ship, then I'm a Chinaman. Hell, the second ship that went down, hit right where I left it. I yelled to you at that time, kid. Couldn't see anything for flames and those damn purple sparks. But what the devil have you been doing?"

Dusty cursed, shrugged.

"Oh well, can't expect everything," he said. "I'll come up and take over and tell you all about it."

"And get my foot in your face!" Curly cracked back. "Tell me later! I'm taking no chances on you. We're going home this time! You and Biff entertain the boy friend."

Tired, hungry, but damned satisfied, Dusty sat down on the steel floor and relaxed. So did Biff Bolton, only he sat on Ekar instead of the floor.

Two hours of mutual silence dragged by, and then a sharp downward motion of the plane brought Dusty to his feet. He leaped for the speaking tube, jiggled the hook.

"Hey, Curly! What the—"

"Keep your pants on, sweetheart!" crackled the earphones. "We're just losing a bit of altitude over Maine. Be landing at Washington in no time. What'll yours be, huh?"

Dusty didn't hear the last. The mention of Washington brought back sharp memory. Jack Horner—General Bradley!

Jerking off the earphones he stepped across the compartment and crouched in front of the broadcasting radio set. Flipping up the contact switch, he spun the wave-length dial to official Intelligence H.Q.

"Calling General Horner!" he barked. "A-Six calling General Horner! Emergency!"

It wasn't two seconds before the speaker unit boomed out the Intelligence chief's voice.

"A-Six! A-Six! Where are you? What—"

"Reporting mission accomplished!" Dusty cut in. "Now flying south—all three of us. Request report on wounded man, please."

"Huh? What's that? Oh yes, yes. He passed the crisis this afternoon. Should be on his feet again in a few weeks. But what have you been doing? Radio H.Q. has picked up God knows how many queer messages. You mean that you've—"

"Yes, sir," Dusty cut in again. Then shooting a side glance at the puffed face of Ekar, "And we're bringing you a souvenir, sir. Not in such hot shape, but it may be useful to you."

"What the hell are you talking about?" the earphones thundered. "No, never mind now. Meet me at the field as quick as you can."

"I'll be there quicker than that, sir," grinned Dusty, "if you'll promise to back me up in a little chat I'm going to have with air force H.Q."

"Yes, yes!" came the booming voice. "I know all about that. You can just forget about it. Only get down here damn quick, and don't break your neck on the way. Understand?"

Dusty said he did, snapped off contact, and went back to the cabin speaker tube.

"Motorman!" he called. "A little more speed! And please wake up my friend and me when we get to Washington!"

The earphones made sound, short and snappy. They said—

"Nerts!"

POPULAR PUBLICATIONS
HERO PULPS

LOOK FOR MORE SOON!

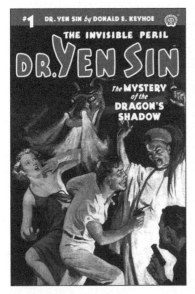